D0020970

Tynse

Wolfgang Hildesheimer

Tynset

Translated by Jeffrey Castle

DALKEY ARCHIVE PRESS

Originally published in German in 1967 by Fischer Bücherei.

Copyright © 1967 Suhrkamp Verlag
Translation © 2016 by Jeffrey Castle

First Dalkey Archive edition, 2016

All rights reserved

The Library of Congress has catalogued this title as LCCN: 201600694

 swiss arts council
prohelvetia

Partially funded by the Illinois Arts Council, a state agency.
Published in collaboration with the Swiss Arts Council, Pro Helvetia, Zurich.

www.dalkeyarchive.com

Victoria, TX / McLean, IL / Dublin

Dalkey Archive Press publications are, in part, made possible through the
support of the University of Houston-Victoria and its programs in creative
writing, publishing, and translation.

Printed on permanent/durable acid-free paper

Translator's Preface

"Thanks to Wolfgang Hildesheimer," Gert Jonke once wrote, "we have now been empowered to transform ourselves into something birdlike, having accomplished which we can imagine ourselves as birdpeople reeling helplessly through the atmosphere or . . . having the mighty pinions of a condor grow from our shoulders, in which latter case, however, we would need to reconcile ourselves to having suddenly turned into eaters of carrion . . ."* While it is possible to ascribe a number of subtexts to this curious assessment, there is clearly a sentiment of appreciation in Jonke's words, recognition of an indebtedness to Hildesheimer (of whom he was an open admirer) for displaying in his writing a sense of freedom, a willingness to break from the constraints of tradition and normalcy in search of new possibilities. Himself a member of the acclaimed *Grazer Gruppe*, an association of Austrian authors known for their often radically experimental methods, Jonke had similar aspirations for his own work, work that can and should be read with Wolfgang Hildesheimer in mind as a predecessor.

Jonke's statement also makes clear that in order to read Hildesheimer's writing—not to mention Jonke's assessment of it—we must be willing to suspend expectations of reality as we know it, or prose as we know it, and to accept the author's imaginative twists and turns as they come. Spontaneously sprouting wings and flying, which actually does happen in a Hildesheimer short story entitled "Why I Changed into a Nightingale,"** is not generally thought to fall within the boundaries of human

* Gert Jonke, "Individual and Metamorphosis," trans. Vincent Kling, *The Review of Contemporary Fiction* 32, no. 2 (Summer 2012), 67.
** Wolfgang Hildesheimer, "Why I Changed into a Nightingale," *The Collected Stories of Wolfgang Hildesheimer*, trans. Joachim Neugroschel (New York: Ecco, 1987), 59–62.

capability—but that is beside the point. The point is this: were we to turn into condors, we would need to come to terms with the new circumstances defining our lives; not only would we be able to fly, but we would also prefer to scavenge. Changes in situation necessitate adaptation. And as Hildesheimer's unapologetic lack of explanation regarding his works' often highly implausible plot developments suggests, it is rarely the goal of his writing to present a faithful picture of conventional reality—or, to put it another way, to be "truthful."

In fact, much of Hildesheimer's work can be said to question and challenge the boundary between truth and fiction, constantly prompting the reader to wonder which is which, and to ponder over the relationship between the two. Perhaps the clearest example of this can be found in *Marbot: A Biography*, one of his better-known works in the English-speaking world. Purporting to bring a long-overlooked figure in English nineteenth-century art and letters back into the public eye, *Marbot* presents a meticulously written and painstakingly researched account of the life of the eponymous art historian, whose radical theories regarding the psychological roots of artistic creation had forced him to the margins of the intellectual community. However, as Hildesheimer later revealed in a letter to the editor of the *London Review of Books*—much to the chagrin of German scholar J. P. Stern, whose review of the work in the same publication not long before had hailed it as an "entirely appropriate" contribution to British intellectual history[*]—Andrew Marbot was actually fictional, and every piece of "authentic" documentation associated with him, down to the shortest diary entry, the result of pure invention.

In his real biography of Wolfgang Amadeus Mozart, which appeared a few years before *Marbot*, Hildesheimer also straddled the line between fact and fiction, weaving lengthy ruminative sections about the composer's psyche, his motivations, his complexes, into the obligatory overview of his life and work. While

---

[*] J. P. Stern, "Sweet Sin," *London Review of Books* 4, no. 14 (August 1982): 3.

technically true to the biographical genre in its inclusion of factual content, upon its release the book drew considerable attention for its unconventional characterization of the famed composer. By repeatedly probing and deconstructing the façade of the carefree boy genius that had been upheld by nearly two centuries of positive, unquestioning reinforcement, Hildesheimer's treatment of Mozart fundamentally altered public perception of one of classical music's most entrenched figures. Even despite their subjective nature, many of the opinions expressed in this work have now been accepted as fact—which in itself is probably the clearest embodiment of what Hildesheimer sought to prove about the fickle nature of truth.

Although *Tynset* (1965), one of two so-called "monologue" pieces in Hildesheimer's *oeuvre*, predates *Mozart* by twelve years and *Marbot* by sixteen, questions about authenticity and authorial truthfulness are still very much in the foreground. Given that the work is admittedly fictional, however, it is not Hildesheimer's truthfulness that is at stake, but that of the narrator, who is also the principal character. The story of *Tynset* revolves around a man of unknown age living in an unknown place, who, as the narration commences, is trying to go to sleep. The ensuing pages chronicle this narrator's digressive thoughts as he alternates between lying in his bed and pacing through his cavernous house, where he occasionally encounters the other members of a very sparse cast of characters: his housekeeper, Celestina, and the ghost of Hamlet's father. From these circumstances alone it is clear that the ruminations of Hildesheimer's restless protagonist are not necessarily to be trusted, or at least cannot necessarily be assumed to be rooted in real events. The reader is often left to wonder at which level of consciousness the narrator's tale is being told. Is it that of a waking person, or that of a dreaming one—or is it perhaps somewhere in between? But then again, who is to say that the narrator's story is not real, and that his experiences are not legitimate? Indeed, this is precisely the paradox of Hildesheimer's writing, and the same characteristic to which Gert Jonke's metaphor of the condor alludes.

This is also what makes the translation of Hildesheimer's work so challenging. To translate a text is, on some level at least, to interpret it, which means that in order to produce something meaningful the translator must fully understand not only the words he or she is translating, but also the intent behind them. Given that one of *Tynset*'s major characteristics is precisely its lack of clarity, its intentional ambiguity, this task becomes a difficult one. Reading through the text, the question I found myself asking the most was to what extent I was actually supposed to understand the narrator's thought processes. Was he hiding things or skewing his story in some way? Or was he even in his right mind while telling it? Correspondingly, some of my most frequent considerations as a translator were whether or not to attempt to clarify moments of confusion, and if I were to try, how to do so without disrupting the work's overall effect.

To find an example of *Tynset*'s intentional ambiguity one need not look farther than the book's opening sentence: "Ich liege im Bett, in meinem Winterbett" [I'm lying in bed, in my winter bed]. What is a winter bed? Does it refer to a specific style of frame, perhaps? Is it particularly warm? Is there a bed for every season? It becomes clear some pages later that the winter bed does indeed have to do with seasons and functions in the life of the narrator as an alternative to the loftier, airier "summer bed" in which he prefers to spend the warm months. As the text progresses, many more, and many considerably stranger, instances of these belatedly explained references crop up, including "the cyclopean room," which is meant to describe the room that houses the narrator's telescope; the frozen body of Chicago evangelist Wesley B. Prosniczer on a snowed-over Alpine pass (a later section reveals that Prosniczer attended a party given by the narrator some time earlier); and perhaps most curious of all, the "Roosters of Attica," which alludes to a time when the narrator snuck into the Acropolis late one night and stirred all of the roosters in the city of Athens with a call. At the point of first mention, each of these references, these "hooks," if you will, is confusing, jarring even, as it comes out of nowhere and seems not to fit in with the narration surrounding it. Its presence encourages skepticism, breeds doubt, and causes the reader to question the work's logic. When its meaning is clarified later, however, the narrative is reconfigured in such a way that the hook makes sense, even if that means proceeding from a rather provisional or even fantastical premise. Like Jonke's birdpeople, who must reconcile being eaters of carrion, the reader is asked to reorient herself in the truth of the moment, to take it on its own terms.

The challenge of translating these hooks into English was to render them in such a way that they were appropriately ambiguous, but also enticing. In most instances this actually involved deviating from the original as little as possible, which is a challenge in itself, as Hildesheimer's German was carefully crafted to elicit this precise effect. One of my most important tasks, then, was to ensure consistency in word choice between often widely separated sections in the text so that the recurrence of key words would serve to jog the reader's memory and facilitate a connection between the introduction of a thread and its eventual development. For example, reusing religiously tinted vocabulary such as "fervent" from Wesley B. Prosniczer's first appearance in the eventual continuation of his story dozens of pages later (where the German *inbrünstig* could yield a variety of English alternatives relating to intense, passionate emotion) serves to hint at the direction the narration is taking before the mention of Prosniczer's name makes it absolutely clear. In other instances, such as in the case of the Roosters of Attica, it was a matter of making small alterations to clarify the hook's function. My addition of "once" to the narrator's original, undeniably cryptic explanation of The Roosters of Attica as "the grand Greek

concert I [once] provoked to overcome my fear" was intended
to frame the reference as anecdotal in some way, hinting at the
possibility of an extended story later on.

It is not only the truth of the narrative, however, that is at
stake in *Tynset*, but the truth of the text itself. In other words,
what kind of text is it? While it would not be unreasonable to
label the work a novel (it is, after all, a fictional work with a dis-
cernible plot and a clear set of characters), Hildesheimer refused
to do so, opting instead to call it a monologue. While perhaps
trivial in some respects (monologic, stream-of-consciousness narration is not exactly a new development in the art of the novel),
this distinction is important in terms of translation because of
its stylistic implications. Is the text to be understood as written,
as a novel would suggest, or spoken, as a monologue would? This
question is further complicated by Hildesheimer's divulgence a
short while after *Tynset*'s publication that the work's structure
is based on a musical rondo (found frequently in Mozart's com-
positions), a form in which a recurring refrain alternates with
contrasting themes—which, it is fitting to note, are frequently
referred to as "digressions." This means that a third medium
must come into consideration: music. Thus, the words filling
Tynset's pages do not only comprise a written text, but a spoken
monologue and a musical composition on top of that.

This compound identity is something I wished to bring out
in my translation, and as such, it stood foremost in my mind
as a determinant of style and voice. While a faithful treatment
of the original German text was enough to preserve the work's
structure as a rondo, I spent considerable effort crafting my
English sentences to strike a balance between the efficiency and
restraint of good writing, the natural flow of spoken language,
and the melody and rhythm of a musical composition. In some
cases, these three facets came neatly together, but in others they
seemed to stand in opposition, forcing me to make choices as to
which should take precedence in the situation at hand. A good
example can be found on page 6–7, where the narrator, riding

on a train, describes the movements of his shadow across an uneven landscape:

und ich sehe mich, mein Bild, meine dunkle Fläche und meine Umrisse, wie sie, weit dort hinten, an den Hängen entlanggetraten oder gezogen oder geschoben werden, durch Gestrüpp, verzerrt, entlang an den Birken und Tannen und über die Felsen und, plötzlich aufrecht und nah und senkrecht, über einen hölzernen Schuppen, und ich sehe mich weit von mir entfernt, sehe mich fern und klein und sehe mich wieder nah und riesig groß und wieder winzig klein, ich bin hier, und ich bin nicht hier, ich bin dort hinten und wieder hier und wieder weit von mir weg.

My translation of this passage reads as follows:

and I see myself, my image, and my dark silhouette as they are dragged, pulled, or pushed along the slopes far below, through underbrush, distorted over birch and pine trees and along the rock face, and then suddenly upright, close, and vertical as we pass a wooden barn. I see myself far away, distant and small, then close and giant, and then tiny again. I am here, I am not here, I am there, and then here again, and once again I am far away from myself.

The German "ich bin" in the final lines translates rather directly to "I am" in English, although English very often contracts these two words to form "I'm." In modern style, this contracted form is much more prevalent than its counterpart, save for in formal settings, where contractions are largely avoided. While not wanting to sound formal, I nevertheless opted to leave the above instances of "I am" open in an effort to preserve the rhythmic quality of Hildesheimer's original. When spoken aloud (as a monologue should be), the two-syllable "I am," which is followed in each instance by another one-syllable word, is strongly evocative of a musical motif—perhaps two sixteenth-note pickups leading to an accented downbeat. The repetition of this motif over the course of the passage's last two lines builds tension and lends the phrase direction, while its final utterance provides cadential closure. Similar considerations came into play in matters of word choice: whereas stylistic conventions in prose might cause one to avoid placing rhymed words in close proximity to one another, I found that judicious use of consonance and assonance lent a musical quality to the text that served to heighten its aural effect.

In conclusion, despite Hildesheimer's penchant for unexpected twists and turns, and his preference for ambiguity in nearly all aspects of writing, I found my work to be the clearest and most effective when I succeeded in embracing these aspects—emphasizing them, even—in an effort to show them for what they are. Translating *Tynset*, like translating any text, was an exercise in balance, in which the decision not to intervene, not to deviate, was as important as the decision to do so. It is my hope that the above discussion will serve not only to illuminate aspects of the translation process for interested readers, but also to elucidate the text itself by clarifying the context from which it arose, in its German and English forms. I wish to extend my deep gratitude to Lauren K. Wolfe as well as the editorial staff at Dalkey Archive Press for their patient and thoughtful guidance as I worked with them to prepare this translation.

Tynset

I'm lying in bed, in my winter bed.

It's time to sleep. But when wouldn't it be? It's quiet. Most nights there's a light wind, accompanied by the crowing of a few roosters. But tonight there is no wind, and not a single rooster is crowing, not yet. Instead, I notice a creaking sound coming from behind the wood-paneled walls—somewhere, the mortar must have split. Buckling first, and then falling away from the frame, ancient cement crumbles into pieces or is pulverized to dust. Or: a crack creeps along a rafter in the ceiling, beginning in one corner and penetrating deep into the other, and then farther, through the wooden wall, following the rafter into the next room, the empty room, where it dwindles and dies away.

The Germans have a saying, *Holz arbeitet*, referring to the gradual loss of substance in wooden structures, which grow smaller and weaker with each passing day. One generally doesn't notice this until many years have gone by, at which point one is inclined to ask—I ask myself, at least—where all of the missing weight has disappeared to, what has become of the substance? I understand that the essential oils evaporate, I know this—but where does their vapor reside? Vanishing matter must vanish to somewhere, must it not? But these are rather inconsequential musings.

At any rate, where there was once substance there is now a yawning emptiness in the form of a cleft, a gap, a crack, or a hole. A door separates ever so slowly from the threshold, a window shrinks from its frame, becoming warped and leaky. And sometimes, a sudden gust of air sweeps through the room, wind, a ball of compacted time, carrying a scent, or perhaps merely the idea of a scent, as if it wanted to awaken a memory. But in reality the wind wants nothing of the sort—quite the opposite,

3

actually. Before having a chance to settle, the idea is swept off, extinguished. It's better that way.

Among the various fleeting aromas that waft by me, a note of incense seems to be the most enduring. Originating in Celestina's room, the scent disperses evenly throughout the entire house. She keeps a small box of it on her dresser, and lights it every night. Where she procures the incense, I'm not entirely sure. Perhaps a devotional shop, I think to myself, if they even do business with secular individuals. No, no, she can't have gotten it there. One would first need to obtain a recommendation, have a consultation, and finally acquire an official signature from at least two clergy members—something she would never be able to manage, not her. Most likely, the incense came from the spice emporium. The scent is not altogether unpleasant; it reminds me of the anticipation leading up to sumptuous wedding dinners— the guests are still in the church, the gratification of indulging the appetite draws closer. It reminds me of a bazaar in the Far East, and of barbaric feasts prepared in the desert. It's curious that these tent dwellers possess such a nuanced understanding of spices. There is another note to the scent as well, perhaps rosemary, or, more likely, oregano. Yes, that's it. Oregano, the softer but wilder variety of marjoram, which I tried to grow once but failed—it seems the plant shall remain untamed. The aroma of incense awakens my appetite, and I have on more than one occasion stolen a small amount of the stuff from Celestina's room and scattered it in the fire before roasting chestnuts—when I used to roast chestnuts, that is.

During the day, the hint of incense is overpowered by other scents, which drift in abundance through my quarters. Short, summery puffs of herbs and spices punctuate longer breezes bearing the aromas of the country: stalls, forests, cattle, neighboring houses and farms. But at night, when the source of the scents is hidden once again, there remains but one fragrance perfuming the air around me: the mild, sweet aroma of holiness, causing me to wander, numb, through my room, a sinful trespasser surrounded by blessings he will never receive.

I reach blindly onto my bedside table in search of something to read and eventually come back with the telephone book, which I set down again.

My second attempt yields a timetable for the Norwegian State Railways from 1963. Not exactly up to date. It is unlikely, however, that a great deal has changed in the railway system during the last few years. No new tracks have been laid, at least not in Europe. Perhaps the occasional crossover line has been added for more convenient connections, saving a few minutes here and there, or even an hour, which elsewhere would have made a significant difference. No more than an hour, though, probably no more than an hour. But when it comes to it, I am not particularly interested in the times. Instead, it is the various places, their distances from one another and from myself, that compel me to read the timetable while lying in bed, far from Norway. Distances always remain the same. This, at least, I can rely on.

The Norwegian timetable is a good timetable. There is not one word, one number, or one symbol too many. Admittedly, the highly beneficial practice of including only essential information is a quality common to other timetables as well. A real timetable offers nothing more than the most pertinent facts and is subjected only to the slightest of changes, mostly on account of the seasons, of which there are only two: summer and winter. No autumn and no spring. Its symbols are simple and accessible, like the illustrations in a children's book. They do not hide from the viewer but serve instead as a gateway to understanding, guiding the eye along crisp lines and tidy rows. Each arrival and departure time is representative of a real, verifiable occurrence: an arrival, a departure. With each line time passes, and the location of the action changes. Correspondingly, each trip serves to confirm the relative reliability of this book, whose singular intention is, after all, to be reliable. Without this, the entire document would be rather senseless, a fact of which the document itself is well aware—

—but the Norwegian timetable contains much more, if one knows how to read it correctly. Between the lines, the great distances unfold into harsh, windy expanses, which the arrival and departure information can only circumscribe, never define or capture. The neatly arranged numbers and symbols merely serve to demarcate the border between one place in the middle of nowhere and another, also in the middle of nowhere, but in a different nowhere where the sayings common to the first place have been modified to the benefit of the second place and the detriment of the first; and in a third place, lying in yet another nowhere, a different saying has taken hold, denouncing as lies the sayings of the first two places—the fourth place is the express train station, from which all sayings have long since departed.

The valleys are hundreds of kilometers long, and in them I can hear the train far off as it traverses the unpopulated, swamp-green highlands. I stand and listen to the distant hissing as it pushes and crawls slowly uphill before crossing over a deep, rocky crevice, where water laps at the walls below. The train's path then tilts slightly as it makes its way down into another valley, cutting between the gray mountain slopes—I hear the echo of the wheels on the tracks,

or better yet: I am standing in the train, in the light of a northern afternoon, between the horizontal rays of a sun that hovers in absolute stillness as it searches for a place to set, a place it will not find for a long time. Shining through the windows and under the line of cars, it casts fleeting silhouettes onto the meadows. Sometimes blurred, sometimes jagged, polygonal, and angular, the shadows reach all the way to the foot of the mountains and occasionally above and beyond,

and I see myself, my image, and my dark silhouette as they are dragged, pulled, or pushed along the slopes far below, through underbrush, distorted over birch and pine trees and along the rock face, and then suddenly upright, close, and vertical as we pass a wooden barn. I see myself far away, distant and small, then close and giant, and then tiny again. I am here, I am not here, I am there, and then here again, and once again I am far away from myself.

I continue reading the timetable. In it, I find a branch line that runs from Hamar to Støren, passing through Elverum, Tynset, and Røros on the way. Despite the melodious timbre of the stops in between, it is the route's secondary character that strikes me. Between the two end stations, both of which are printed in bold, the three fine-print names in the middle appear rather sullen, like neglected children who have not lived up to expectations, like disappointments, cowering in the shadow of the distinguished parents looming on either side: Støren, the blonde mother, Hamar, the dark-haired father. It all sounds a bit like a sorrowful fairy tale, something told around the fireplace as the embers slowly die away.

Røros. I believe I've seen a picture of it once. It lies there like a final encampment on the path leading to the end of the earth, before the path loses itself in regions so inhospitable, so threatening, that expeditions to them are postponed year after year. Because of this the town has become a sort of "eternal autumn settlement," if you will, its population comprised mostly of researchers in their twilight years, whose lofty ambitions have long since dwindled, and who are now slowly falling into obscurity. They spend their days in Røros searching for the geographical origins of a northern brand of melancholia—the southern variant has long since been uncovered and thoroughly analyzed—a melancholia that has been sought for quite some time without success, even though it has and will continue to inhabit the nooks and crannies of the old wooden houses and the arid gardens that lie untended behind them. Like a wind that is neither cold nor warm, it blows, unnoticed, through the

streets. I see it blowing. Far off in the distance, an early winter
creeps over the forests from its hiding place behind the heavy
sky. But the people here are prepared. There wasn't a train station in the picture; it was hopeless, inescapable. But there were
telephone poles.

Elverum and Tynset, however, are two places I know nothing
about, but even so, they appear promising. Elverum, due to its
neutral -*um* ending, perhaps slightly less so than Tynset. Yes,
Tynset because of the *y*. In places with a *y*, it's not uncommon
to uncover secrets, even if in the end they are often nothing
more than myths. But Tynset does not sound like mythology,
at least not as much as Røros does. Had I never seen the picture,
the name would have evoked an island, on whose shores a god's
beloved was born from the sea foam but had long since been
swallowed up again by the waves, consumed by her thirst for
immortality.

And then there is Hamar. I've been to Hamar—purely by
chance, like so many other places. Was I alone? Yes, I was alone.
If memory serves, I was coming from Lillehammer. Hamar has
a railway museum, but I did not visit it. The reason why not
escapes me, for I am on the whole quite interested in trains. I
remember the iron streetlamps and a pleasing, but not particularly noteworthy, appearance: deserving of a postcard, but not
two. A place where very little has been, and where not much is
expected to come. At the same time, it's not a place you would go
out of your way to avoid. A bishop's see: a place where the bishop
seems almost omnipresent, lurking in the faded, pigeon-soiled
brownstone of an accomplished, forward-thinking predecessor,
who even played soccer, and who led the church in a new direction; in the penetrating eyes behind hard, stiff metal-framed
glasses in a room enclosed by tightly drawn curtains; in the gaze
of an innkeeper who is proud of the fact that no mischief ever
takes place under his watch. But even Hamar is not without its

secrets, lying there among the mountains, trees, and boulders, the whole of it loosely assembled from wood and stone—never marble—with its railway museum and train station and its main line south toward Oslo, with connection to Göteborg, and north toward Trondheim, and then farther, far past the Arctic Circle, the secondary line to Støren via Elverum, Tynset, and Røros, as well as a few other spur lines that disappear in steep curves (curves that sweep upward, as only railway workers are capable of constructing them, for only they know the lay of the land) deep into the pine forests toward who knows where. Back then, it was likely November or October, all lines ran directly into the fog, meaning that my train must have passed through it as well on the way from Lillehammer, on a route whose shape is not entirely dissimilar to a question mark. Perhaps it is merely on account of murkiness and spur lines that this place, now, after the fact, appears not to be without its secrets. Indeed, as I study this picture, searching for its components and piecing them together, its contours, its content, and its color begin to fade. Even today, I remain critical of these images. And perhaps that's it: one must work carefully to determine what is a secret and what is merely fog. Perhaps I should try to erect a barrier against the fog, once and for all.

That reminds me: a while ago, I read about the death of a famous Wagnerian soprano in the newspaper—I have since forgotten which one, but it's not really that important. Unless you are a professional in the field, they are very difficult to tell apart—one is just like the other, they all hit Sieglinde's high C♯ effort-lessly, yes, this is the bar by which they are all measured, C♯ is the determining factor, their salaries stand in direct correlation to the amount of breath they are able to reserve for this one note—anyways: this particular singer, whose first name was Karin, or Kerstin or Kirsten or Karstin or Karsten, was born in Hamar, and if I am not mistaken, to a musical family with very modest means—her father sang for a living as well—to parents who recognized her talent early and provided endless support, despite the considerable financial burden such an upbringing entails. Throughout her career, she would always think fondly of her childhood home, and so on and so forth, something like that, I believe, or that's the general idea at least. The recently deceased singer has added yet another tiny detail to the many insignificant characteristics of this town, but not a good one, I'm afraid. Because of her, Hamar is now on the horizon, if only as a tiny blip, for an entire wave of headhunters from Bayreuth, Vienna, and New York—caught in a periodic sidelong glance, the object of secret observation, a marginal note in deliberations about roster problems. I don't like this term very much, but there you have it: roster problems. These days I believe there are over ten thousand different kinds of problems. Thus, Hamar has managed to garner a certain amount of attention for itself. The growth of natural talent signifies fertile ground, and the possibility that there might be others as well, who could emerge at any time. There really isn't anything to do about this, but even if there were, I doubt there would be anybody to do it.

Enough about Hamar. Is there anything else to say? I don't believe so. Wait, yes there is. During the last war, a German captain had thirteen of the town's residents hanged from lamp-posts. Originally there had been seventeen selected for this fate, but the captain was in a hurry and, in anticipation of the orders he was sure to receive later, ended up shooting the last four on his own. Other than that, there really isn't anything more to say about Hamar—bishop's see, spur lines, railway museum, lamp-posts, Wagner singers—no, nothing else, that's it. This place has nothing else to offer.

It is late. I want to try to sleep, but something has roused me. I have already forgotten what it was, and I will try not to remember; I will try to glide peacefully onto new tracks and think about other things in the hopes that they do not also contain secrets that will wake me once again. It is still too early for a walk through the house—that comes later, if I still can't sleep. I must be judicious with my nightly activities, save them for later if at all possible. Yes, I will get up later and walk through the house again.

During the night, I get up several times, and at least one of those times I go walking through the house, passing through the cavernous wooden room, whose silence is like a sustained fermata, interrupted on occasion by the various noises coming from the wood, and the babbling of the fountain. From there I go through the library, sometimes pausing at the walls of books—sometimes not—before continuing to the stone staircase, where, when it isn't too dark, I encounter Hamlet's father—

he stands up top, on the highest stair, and looks down at me with a note of idle expectation in his eyes, waiting for me to come to him, to kneel down, and to kiss his hand, establishing a relationship that will eventually end with him taking me as his son, for his own son was a disappointment. This is what he is waiting for, the old warrior. He looks at me as if to say I owe him something, but he is mistaken—I do not owe him anything. I will not make him aware of his mistake, however, for doing so would establish a relationship, and then he would have won.

Past this gaze, past these eyes, I slip under his deadened glances and continue into the storage room in back, the cyclopean room, where spices are hung to dry in the summer and autumn months. It smells good here. Sometimes I climb up to the telescope—sometimes not—before leaving again and continuing on into the kitchen—or maybe not—and then back up the stairs. Upon reaching the second floor, I look into each of the four rooms, one of which houses my sprawling summer bed.

This is where I sleep in the summer, elevated, airy, and sublime, enclosed by wood in an emptiness that rustles with silence. This is the point of departure for my summer-night wanderings, but in the winter I spend very little time here. In the colder months I prefer a different room, one that is full of objects—to find it I must go back downstairs. I never go higher than the second floor, especially not at night. This is not because of Hamlet's father, however, who more often than not has vanished by the time I return, leaving nothing but a thin column of injured pride behind. No, not because of him. I do not go higher because there is only one room on the top floor: Celestina's room, and I never enter it. From below, I often hear her snoring, or I hear nothing, which means she is sitting in front of a bottle of red wine, or that she has taken the bottle with her to bed and is drinking it there. Other times I hear mumbling, which means she is praying.

Celestina drinks a lot and prays a lot. She drinks because she drinks, and she prays because she believes in God and is pious— no, no, it's not quite that simple, not quite so unequivocal: her thirst for wine had to have begun at some point, just like her thirst for God. But unlike an acquired taste, with which no individual is born, unlike the longing that is reared and nourished and then suddenly crystallizes as conviction, bearing fruit in the form of fear and indulgence and settling around the organs and the senses as a hard, impenetrable crust, the root of Celestina's desire for wine lies elsewhere, in a secret that will likely never disclose itself to me. I have a suspicion that she is an escaped nun. I might be mistaken—I have never asked her, and I never will ask her, which means I will never find out whether it is true, nor will I ever know whether it was the desire to drink that drove her from the convent or whether she started drinking in an attempt to expunge the shame of leaving (or perhaps another sin, perhaps even a mortal sin) from her thoughts. In any event, she is now irrevocably trapped in a vicious circle, which, once closed, cannot be broken out of again. Come morning, she's never in a state of mind that would permit her to attend Mass, and each day becomes a wellspring of fresh guilt. As the guilt spreads, it feeds upon her soul, making it lame, and drives her body to harder and harder labor in an effort to suppress the shame festering inside. Succumbing fully to the strength of her impulse, she presses on with great ardor and her achievements are exemplary. In the afternoon, her physical strength begins to wane, making room for the old feelings of guilt to return, unmuted, immutable, bringing with them the thirst for wine and forgiveness that cannot be stilled; and it is with greater and greater frequency that she interrupts her labors—wherever she may be: in church, in her room, in the garden, or in the yard—to have a drink or to pray, or to do both simultaneously; and it is in this manner that she staggers through the afternoon, with increasing effort, until she is no longer able to attend the evening Vespers. Sometimes she tries, but her legs cannot carry her and she quickly turns around, resolving instead to pray at home, this time without drinking. But when the words inevitably escape her and the spirit of the scripture remains distant, she sinks once again into bed, bottle in hand, forgetting in the ensuing stupor to recite the rosary, the final opportunity for reconciliation with her creator, who made her into a drinker in the first place. During the night she wakes up, fills her thurible with incense, lights it, and prays and drinks and prays and drinks and lies down once again and sinks into an inebriated slumber from which she will awaken too late and miss morning Mass, defeated and destroyed.

Celestina doesn't go to church anymore but instead spends her days writhing in sin, persecuted and suffocated by the booming of the bells that will one day run her into the ground, haunted by the unrelenting gaze of the priest, trapped in the clutches of chubby hands and pointy fingers that grope under her dress to palpate her sins, engorging them for the day of reckoning. The iron lattice slides back, and there he sits: red cheeks, hefty chin, and a massive gut, fingering an absolution in the deep pockets of his robes. I wish I were able to help her, but I am not. I would happily bear some of her guilt, for I carry very little of my own, very little. But Celestina, she relinquishes nothing, no: she wishes to shoulder her burden alone, which, in the end, she is perfectly entitled to do. And who knows? Perhaps a stroke of recompense, an unexpected bit of justice is awaiting her somewhere in eternity. Only a bit, though. But even if she did allow it, I wouldn't know how to take her burden upon myself—this is not something I've ever had to do before.

Sometimes, when I enter one of my rooms, I am greeted by the subtle aroma of incense, and of wine and wax. The furniture has been freshly polished, everything is tidy, organized, and clean—except for one corner, where a pillow with two knee-shaped impressions is lying on the floor, next to it a glass with a few lingering red drops: remnants of the recent consecration. And somewhere, in a corner hidden from sight, the vacuum cleaner attachment is lurking, tainting the otherwise rigorous purity of the scene laid out before me.

It's time to sleep—I lay the timetable back down onto my night-stand. Yes, I was coming from Lillehammer that time. What I did there, I no longer remember. I do, however, seem to recall that Lillehammer is home to a factory that produces high-quality briar pipes: first the burl wood must collect on the forest floor, until it is ancient, hard as stone, having not been borne by a tree for hundreds of years—it comes from the Mediterranean to the far north, where it is sawn, cut, burned, blown, lathed, stained, spiced, polished, and finally savored. A few of these exquisite pieces have made it back down into the south, enriched by their northerly winter excursions. I bought my burl pipe from Lillehammer in Bologna—unexpected connections always turn up somewhere, but attempts to trace them very often lead to disorientation and disappointment.

Tynset. The sound lingers.

It sounds bright, glassy—no, that's not right, it sounds metallic. The letters are well chosen, they fit together. Or does it just seem that way? No, they fit together, I would love to name a place like this, a place in Norway to be sure, but somewhere far removed from this station on the branch line from Hamar to Støren. But there is nothing left for me to name anymore, everything already has a name, and whatever doesn't, well, it doesn't exist. No: there are many names for things that don't exist.

Tynset: it is a place I lingered in passing, that is circled, encircled, by my thoughts. This *y*! Reaching down below the line (truly a letter between the lines) and diagonally to the left, it extends its claw to catch passing thoughts as they float by—tired, and increasingly likely to stumble upon, or even welcome a hindrance—and rips them apart, bits and chunks clinging to its black surface.

But this *y* isn't even pronounceable. At the very least it is by sheer coincidence that the mouth happens to achieve just the right position in order for the voice to sound it correctly. This, along with the *y*'s slant, separates it from all other letters, an elusive presence among concise facts. In the mouth, upsilon lies on the path from *i* to *ü*, right in the middle, but *ü* also lies at a midpoint, precisely halfway between *i* and *u,* a journey whose distance is twice as long. The second half of this route, from *ü* to *u*, has no middle point, or rather no symbol to mark it. Here there is nothing, just silence, in the truest sense of the word, the unspeakable; this is where it begins, barely apparent in the most inconspicuous of things, growing larger and more apparent until suddenly it is immeasurable, horrible, unspeakable.

However, when I really think about it—when I try to find my way in this cloud of ruminations—when I study the name Tynset not just from below, but from all sides, I come to the conclusion that its allure is not confined to the letters that comprise it: the *y* serves merely to ensnare the gaze, while the other letters act as a latticed screen, behind which the true secret lurks. But the secret is nowhere close to being uncovered, and the riddle nowhere near being solved. If I separate the word into its two syllables, I first get "Tyn," a high-pitched gong note, the beginning of a ritual in a temple, empty save for the presence of a single celebrant, sunken deep within himself, far away, farther even than Greece, where, by the way, it is still possible to find people capable of pronouncing *y* correctly—so first I have "Tyn," which is jerked abruptly from its resonating trance by "set," much in the same way that a resounding cymbal crash is reduced instantaneously to silence by the short, deft movement of a single, agile finger: Tynnn-Settt.

Earlier, when I used to live in the city—and in Germany—I would occasionally take pleasure in reading through the phone book. Like the train schedule, the phone book also possesses a distinct worth—although only to a certain degree—that surpasses its absolute value as a functional item. It is a book that, on the whole, wastes no time, a book full of compacted information and facts—never does it venture into the realm of speculation—and yet here as well there appears to be something between the lines, something that tells a story, a company nameplate, embossed copper on a marble doorway, which in reality represents nothing more than a failing entrepreneur's final, futile attempt at a life of glamour, or perhaps his corrupt brother's hopes for reliable income. Here and there I also detected a hint of pointless exertion, a subscriber's desire to free himself from monotonous particulars, to cast off his number and replace it with something altogether unheard of—even if not miraculous, then perhaps a step closer to it, and by "it" I mean a miracle.

In any case, compared to the timetable, the phone book does not present an exhaustive account of its subject—no, that's not right, I'm not expressing myself correctly: compared to the timetable, which presents a complete picture of a vast organization in its entirety, namely the infrastructure upon which people are transported from one point to another via train, the telephone book does not adequately represent the sheer enormity of the network to which it is tied: the city. Yes, that's it: the documentation is incomplete, there are gaping holes in which

the telephone-less are hiding, tiny holes in the third floor of a
building on the brink of condemnation, crumbling, decaying,
yellowing; there are larger holes, forgotten scraps from deceased
bread-winners, and giant holes left by entire streets, whose
blatant, disarming squalor leeringly stretches out an ulcerous
hand to demand payment for each glance upon its disfigured
countenance. Also absent from this account is the mischievous
grin of an unlisted number, the averted gaze of an outsider who
scorns the device on principle, and the vanity of the refined
misanthrope, who has long since rid his abode of all forms of
communication, congratulating himself on a newly achieved
level of disdain—all of these cases have escaped the ink-stained
fingers of the Communications Department.

All in all, then, not much more than a boring, sad piece of
reading material, evoking very little, and relaying nothing more
than what is already known, worn out, forgotten, repressed;
illuminated windows of high buildings, and behind them the
dramas of unfaithfulness, legacy hunting, a painstakingly
crafted murder, courtyard gates, lighted for the convenience of
the guests, the guests themselves, back entryways for service
workers, the workers themselves, metal gates to keep out the
salesmen, but no salesmen of course; sterile, foreboding waiting rooms where death plays its merciless game of selection,
and death itself, rows of reception desks and behind them the
quiet footsteps of malice, with thinning hair and sleeve guards,
in front of them the shaky conscience of the intimidated tax
evader, accustomed to playing the intimidator because he does
it elsewhere, the ridiculous false secrets hidden behind lines of
symbols and codes, concocted by agencies and firms—"industry
language," as they call it—the night guard keeping watch over
the pharmacy, the blue light of the nocturnal hours flickering
softly in patients' rooms, where not a single life can be saved if
it has already been forfeited; the frowning and head shaking
of officials clad in white coats, the nighttime police searches,
racing to uncover an act of desperation, the retired criminal,

surrounded by children, grandchildren, and a statute of limitations, closed doors, a final disagreement, false hopes, outrage, sorrow, fear.

Still, I could not deny myself the opportunity to pick up the telephone from time to time and make a call. I needed proof of the book's reliability, I wanted to hear the voices, the names. It was a test that always ended in positive affirmation—I had never expected anything else—at least insofar as the information in the book corresponded to the numbers and names of the speakers on the other end. In another sense, however, this practice proved to be most unsatisfying, namely because the recipients of my inquiries were often not disposed, or in some cases not even able—given that I always called during the time they had allotted for sleeping—to present themselves in a manner consistent with their portrayal in the phone book. As might be expected from such circumstances, I was rarely able to move those I called to reveal any true part of their identities.

While thumbing through the phone book one particular night, I came upon the inhabitant of a house that stands diagonally across from my own. I never knew him. I think he was named Huncke or something like that. I called him; it was quite late at night. A light came on in a second-floor window, and immediately thereafter, he picked up. At first he didn't want to reveal his name. Come to think of it, I don't even remember why I cared to find out in the first place. My tone and words were those of a concerned, well-meaning citizen, who wanted nothing but the best for the individual he was trying to reach; this meant, of course—surely he would understand—that I first needed to be certain I was speaking with the person for whom my good intentions were meant. This seemed to make sense to him; in all honesty it probably would have made sense to me as well, especially when presented with such care. He gave me his name, and with that, my goal had been achieved. All of a sudden, though, this one victory was not enough. I wanted to hear more, to delve into the unknown.

I said, "So you are Mr. Huncke," to which he replied "Yes . . . why?" but almost as if he himself were no longer convinced of the veracity of his answer. As I searched for a suitable reply, he asked another question: "What is this about?" Behind a veil of probably quite justified hostility, I heard a sensitive conscience begin to tremble, but an answer to his question evaded me. What was this about? I wanted to know something. I was awake, interested. So I asked, in a voice that seemed friendly to me, "Do you feel guilty, Mr. Huncke?" Were I the recipient of such a question, I would surely have answered "no"—even to the most foreign, unknown individual, my reply would unequivocally have been: "No, I don't." But Huncke was different. There was an audible quivering in his voice as he spoke—his guilt had been awakened, and was growing, multiplying at an immeasurable rate. He hissed back at me: "Just you wait! We'll be back soon! And when we are, you'll get yours!"

I don't know whom he meant by "you." In any case, this was an entirely new experience, whose freshness endowed me with a sense of superiority—I was master of my intent. As I spoke, my voice was powerful, it reverberated through the night, making a telephone all but unnecessary for reaching my neighbor at this late hour: "Mr. Huncke, please listen to me now: they know everything, everything. Do you understand? I would advise you to leave now, while you still have time!" He hung up, I hung up, and immediately thereafter a second window was illuminated, followed by another, and then another until the entire building was glowing like an opera house at intermission. Barely half an hour after our conversation had concluded, a taxi arrived, and the victim of my call exited the house with two suitcases under his arm. He loaded his things, got in, and the taxi drove off. Whether Mr. Huncke was leaving a wife behind him, I do not know. What is clear is that he did not bring her along, and neither she nor any other individual bothered to turn out the lights in the house. The building remained lit for the rest of the night, as well as the next. But then it became dark again, and stayed dark—at least as long as I lived across the way.

Since then, I have repeated this game on a few different occasions. Of course, I have no way of knowing whether my successes endured past the initial moment of departure, whether my victims continued to proceed according to the directions whispered to them over the nighttime wires by the temporary administrator of their conscience. Distance made continued oversight next to impossible. Only in one of these instances was I completely sure of victory: One night, as I perused the telephone book, I came upon a certain Gottfried Malkusch, owner of a printing business. I decided to give him a call. The telephone was picked up immediately, and a name supplied without hesitation. Obviously, he had been expecting to be contacted, despite the hour. This time, I decided to take a more direct approach and whispered my warning breathlessly into the receiver: "Mr. Malkusch, they know everything." After a second, he replied hoarsely: "No." "Yes," I said back, "I'm afraid they do." "So they know everything." "Everything," I repeated, this time in a more friendly tone, like a confidant whose life had been equally impacted by the news. "And now?" he asked. "Malkusch," I whispered kindly, for I did in this moment feel a certain pity for the man, "Malkusch, you should leave before it's too late!" Another helpless pause, and then: "Do I have time to pack a few things?" "I'm afraid not," I whispered. Suddenly, my empathy had vanished. "No, Malkusch, I wouldn't if I were you." "Thank you, Obwasser," he said. Yes, "Obwasser." Then he hung up— and I am fairly certain he did not pack anything.

I had two other nighttime conversations with residents in my vicinity. I needed to run more tests. The names of those I spoke with are long forgotten. One of them, who lived directly across from me, only whispered, despite the fact that a radio or turn-table was playing the *Eroica* in the background the entire time. This one did not turn on any lights—the house remained completely dark save for the glow of a flashlight, darting from floor to floor behind the windowed façade, from the attic all the way down to the basement. Around an hour after the conversation had ended, he came out of the front door in a jacket and hat, carrying with him a violin case. Upon entering the garden, he produced a long-ish object from his pocket and buried it with his hands. Wiping himself off with a handkerchief, he walked to the mailbox, took a letter from his jacket, and inserted it into the slot. He stood for a while on the edge of the street, glancing from side to side, as if the choice of direction were proving difficult. Finally, he made up his mind and set off, and with each subsequent step, his posture seemed to regain its former confidence as a new goal began to take shape ahead of him.

The second of these conversations was with a neighbor of mine. In this case I was not able to see what happened, but I sensed a growing unrest in the adjacent house. No voices or words, no slamming of doors. There was simply an aura of agitation behind the walls, allusions to dampened warnings, orders given in a hiss, final accusations before separation, accepted between bouts of sobbing, followed by the quiet click of the front door, the loud squeaking of the garage, rendering void all previous attempts at caution, the stubborn, resentful sputtering of the engine—he was leaving in his own car—and then, a few minutes later, a shrill, piercing scream from the house: "Artur! Artur!" I cannot be sure exactly for whom the screaming was intended. Perhaps it was the result of a parallel occurrence that had nothing to do with the chain of events I had set into motion. After all, the man I had warned was not named Artur. His name, which I have just now remembered, was Erhard. Erhard Selbach. His number was six-zero-seven-four-four. How absurd our memories are!

Now he's crowing, the rooster. Twice, three times. The friend I wait for all night, who animates the silent hours, my companion, my loyal, faraway ally.

He lives on a neighboring farm. In actuality, his voice is much more reminiscent of the singsong of nursery rhymes than most rooster calls I have heard, and I have heard many. Almost as if he were modeled after the rooster one always finds in children's books. *Ki-ki-ri-Ki!* The first three syllables are of equal strength, followed by a pronounced accent on the fourth, which is prolonged by a fermata. After a proper sustain, the note begins a gradual diminuendo, and eventually fades away to nothing. In fact, it would not be a far cry to liken the rooster's call to Beethoven's Fifth, both in terms of rhythm as well as the sheer pathos it exudes. As morning approaches, he often becomes hoarse, but rarely does this lead to a reduction in volume. Sometimes, when the wind is blowing from the southeast, I hear a second rooster answering him. The origin of the reply is significantly farther away: when I do manage to hear it, it is soft—barely audible between the gusts of wind that carry it—and quickly dissipates again, like a cap of foam between two waves. Whenever I can't sleep, I can hear the rooster—or roosters, if the wind is right—crowing throughout the night, but they don't bother me. When I do sleep, they don't awaken me, and when I wake up, they don't provide comfort. The notion that roosters only begin their crowing at daybreak, accompanying the sun's ascent from behind the horizon, is, as I have gradually come to understand, nothing more than a myth perpetuated by poets—although in truth it is one of their smaller lies. Confronted by the vast expanse of the nighttime hours, I have taken to counting the seconds between the call of one rooster and the answer of the other. The length of the pauses is always different, and sometimes the answer is so late that I begin to wonder whether the two birds are really connected at all, whether they are even able to hear each other. Perhaps it is only me who experiences both of them, the silent, passive connection between two creatures relegated to the solitude of night, each crying for himself in his own dark space, which is separated from all other spaces by the density of blackness.

But no: despite the distance, these two birds have united to overcome together the fear and loneliness that keeps them awake while their hens sleep or lay their nightly eggs. Their fear endows them with a certain sense of worth, a nocturnal pride they do not feel during the daytime hours. For when it is light, when they stumble on swollen, stumpy legs through a sea of hens, selecting one at random for the tedious ritual of copulation, they are utterly bereft of pride. Comforted by the grandeur of the nighttime herald, these creatures possess a masculine ridiculousness.

As the night approaches, feelings and urges gradually diminish, giving way to a human brand of fear. Standing his ground, alone on the farm, my rooster forms a union with another, and together they face the darkness—most likely there are others that join the duet as well, others I cannot hear, ever-widening circles, rings of roosters extending for miles and miles. Yes, I am sure, in fact, that this happens, and has been happening ever since I heard The Roosters of Attica, the grand Greek concert I once provoked to overcome my own fear.

Fear? Yes, fear of the silence of the nights, when the shapes are up and about, the shapes that feel no fear.

Today the fear set in after I withdrew from these shapes. I didn't really withdraw from them, though—it was more that I retreated farther away than I already was, that I fled to a different country. When I say "fled" I am not referring to the few who actually listened to my telephone warnings and left. They all had something on their conscience, which makes them much preferable to those who lack any conscience whatsoever. During the time when I was making the calls, my thoughts accompanied many a victim on his journey. These days, however, I feel that the company of my thoughts provided too heavy a counterpoint to the hastily whistled marching tune befitting such an escape. I saw—it's almost ridiculous—I saw my victims at some sort of crime scene, cowering with guilt before a shattering realization, or in the barren emptiness of the desert, barefooted, treading the path of purification in a hairshirt, while in reality they were sitting at some bar drinking a beer or perhaps some champagne— yes, that's it: of course they were drinking champagne, whiling away their shiny new lives with shiny new lovers. I don't know if or when my victims returned, but their quick action upon my calling suggests that these men were comfortable anywhere: regardless of the location, they could hammer in their stakes and build a new existence. Masters of their fate, and in most cases the fates of others as well. In all probability, I did not reach any of them in their first lives. Instead, my calls served to evoke a memory, which, despite being a small triumph, is a triumph nonetheless, for it is a memory they had been trying to erase.

Of a different sort were the two men without fear, who did not try to erase anything; the last two calls, first a warning, then a threat, and with it an abrupt end to the conversation, and to a phase in my life.

When I came across the name Obwasser in the phone book I was reminded of my conversation with Malkusch, who had mistaken me for Obwasser. I decided to test the likeness. It was around midnight when I gave him a call, but he picked up immediately. "Karl Dietrich Obwasser," he said, the last two syllables in an ascending glissando. The question sounded rather self-important, as if it anticipated an unworthy answer, and it is a mystery to me how anybody, especially a co-conspirator like Malkusch, could possibly mistake my voice for his. I whispered: "Obwasser, listen closely . . ." but he interrupted: "Who is this? Skowronek?"—"No," I said, with skillfully insinuated impatience, "not Skowronek . . ."—"Oh: Dönitz!"—"No," I said

again, "it's Malkusch!"—"Malkusch?" he said, his voice now
hasty and muted, "I thought you were already . . ."—"Not yet,"
I said, "not yet. But they're after me, and you too, Obwasser.
They know everything, do you understand? Everything!" At this
point, Obwasser's voice lost the pomp with which it had begun
the conversation, and suddenly I understood how it was possible for Malkusch to have mistaken my voice—or anyone's for
that matter—for his. "Depot Eighteen as well?"—"It's well past
that now," I said, "Depot Nineteen."—"That just isn't possible,
Malkusch," whispered Obwasser. "And Twenty," I whispered.
That was my mistake. I don't think I would have uncovered
a large secret, but perhaps something small, something worth
knowing purely on account of how paltry it was. After a short
pause, Obwasser responded with brooding but controlled suspicion: "Who is this?" I hung up.

The last one was Kabasta. Today I can no longer muster the
courage to call him, and the hope of awakening even the slightest sense of unrest in this man has long since faded. He was the
only true player in my game, and also the only one of whose
existence—a terrible one, at that—I had been aware beforehand,
and whom I had actually seen. It was somewhere, in some small
village where he had been serving on the district council, in
a tavern—no, that's not right. I was definitely eating outside.
He was seated at a neighboring table, part of a hunting club,
laughing, broad shouldered men dressed entirely in green and
surrounded by greenery. Panting dogs at their side, they drank
beer and schnapps and ate something that looked positively
horrifying, a plate of slaughtered animals: pickled pig kidneys,
blood sausage, and the like. He was telling a long story from
the war in the East, or maybe in the West, and found numer-
ous opportunities to raise his right arm and show off his hand,
which, when splayed out, boasted alternating patches of red and
pale yellow. He kept saying things like: "with this hand," or:

"with my hand here," but I was never able to make out what came after; the emphasis on "this hand" was too strong. As he spoke, the hand continued to get larger and redder.

I called him at two in the morning. Like many of the others, he picked up almost immediately; his voice was indignant: "What is it now?" Apparently, I was not his first caller that night—somebody, probably some subordinate from the office, had disturbed him a short while before. I think, however, that Kabasta rather likes being disturbed, for only then is he in his element, on a mission, keeping watch, especially at night, when it is his duty to survey the channels of insubordination, to feel, to listen, to spy on potential insurgents scheming to undermine one of his many directives. "Is this Doctor Kabasta?" I asked. "Is that you again, Oscoćil?" he asked me—there it was again, this incomprehensible mix up. It seems never to occur to anybody that the unimaginable could happen, even if the unimaginable is something as insignificant as a nighttime call from a stranger. "No," I said, "no, Doctor, it's not Oscoćil this time, it's Bloch." The name just came to me, it didn't mean anything in particular—at least not at this point. "Who?" "Bloch," I said, "and I'm calling to tell you that they know everything . . ." I listened to my voice as it trailed off, but no answer came. I heard him breathing, I saw his eyes getting smaller, saw his large red and yellow hand as it reached for a pen, careful not to make any noise. ". . . and I would advise you to leave while there's still time." I heard his silence, I heard the note he was making to himself on the pad of paper: "Bloch," another entry in a long list of names, some of them crossed out, erased, closed cases, former disturbers of the peace, tracked down once and for all by a practiced hunter, equally aware of his own immortality as of the mortality of his victims. I heard him writing, I heard as he lay down his pen, and I heard his search for an excuse to keep me on the telephone longer. "One moment," he said. I was surprised that Kabasta couldn't think of anything better. "One moment." I heard him pick up another receiver with his other hand, the large red and yellow one, quietly lay it down, and dial a number. The first rotation was long, zero. It had to be the police. I hung up, and from that moment on I felt persecuted—not necessarily unjustly so, for I was not entirely without fault, especially considering my status as a public threat. This, however, is not a perspective I am used to adopting, and certainly not one I would ever choose to honor.

The next day there was a crackling when I picked up the telephone. That night I did not make any calls, and on the following day two technicians came by. They told me my telephone wasn't working, and that they would have to take a look at it. They examined it, and afterwards it looked different. I could not have said how it looked different after the inspection—its color and shape were unchanged. But it stood out from the rest of my room now, it caught my gaze, conspicuously inconspicuous, like an evil bud from which horror is waiting to blossom. I stopped using it, stopped answering; when it rang, I didn't want to give a name, not mine or anybody else's, I didn't want to betray my voice, didn't even want to lay down and go to sleep next to the blasted thing. Shortly thereafter I left that house, the town as well, and the state, and moved here. That was eleven years ago.

And here, still standing next to this bed, my winter bed, is my telephone of eleven years. Only the receiver does me any good these days, the mouthpiece has become superfluous. There are not many—not anymore—who would think to call me, and every call I get turns out to be a wrong number. I myself do not make any calls either—I don't know whom I would speak with or what I would say. As far as the other person goes, I either already know how they would answer or I don't care to. I have even stopped calling strangers. I don't hunt for guilt anymore, I am no longer a persecutor. I have been warned.

I use the telephone only to listen, sometimes just to the humming silence, the only noise made by the passing time. I listen,

listen through the wires and beyond them into the room, and then outwards, over the fields to the far corners of the Earth, my ear glides above the seas, I feel myself in cables and poles and waves, listening for something to appear or to disappear—but sometimes to hear something in words as well, something that takes place outside of my room, outside of my house, preferably outside of the Earth, over it, over the plains, the mountains, and the seas, in the atmosphere—a weather report, for instance, or as they call it, the weather forecast, I enjoy hearing it; even if the words are not always clear or well chosen, the weather forecast opens up an entire panorama of possibilities before me, there are still possibilities up here—true, this is no cosmic panorama, I do not hear the tones of the sun, the whispers of the Crone, or the cold silence of the moon. There is no wind from other planets, like there is up there on the telescope's wooden casing. But yes, even here I ascend above myself, above the Earth's surface, I drift, begin to trace a path, I float—

sail, like a billowing cumulus cloud, or high, flitting, and erratic like a cirrus, or perhaps I am a nimbus, a dense fibrous emulsion fleeing from the powerful, massive deep of the Atlantic toward the coastline, where I dissolve and scatter; I am air in the wake of a departing night—

or an island of storms, ruling over the mountains, sailing by night over the glaciers, catching and tearing on icy peaks, or

—alternatively: from the south, coming from the south, from above, a malicious down-slope wind, a foehn. I dive heavily down toward the earth, and can feel myself in the heads of those I thrash, as I, now one of them, am thrashed as well. I ricochet off of the steep southern hillsides and collide with other masses, masses of cool Scandinavian air, harbingers of polar streams—a battle in the atmosphere; the weather swells upward and sends discharges down to the earth, and there I lie, here, under the refreshing discharge—

—I dial 6-1-6, and immediately recognize the well-groomed female voice with its over-enunciated diction. She says: *aside from some mild winds from east to northeast, remaining quite pleasant overall, especially in the northern lowlands*—quite pleasant overall. Pleasant, that never means anything other than a cloudless, sunny sky. Sometimes, in summer, the sky remains cloudless for weeks on end, its blue growing deeper and deeper as the sun singes, burns, and dries, and the earth turns to a cracking crust, but the weather is pleasant, a nice day to die—*in the midlands, however, the fog line is expected to remain at 800 meters*—the fog line, there it is, the long-awaited fog line—*air pressure in northern Europe has risen in recent days, but fallen in the south and over the Mediterranean, which means we can expect*—there they are, the invisible battles in the air, playing out above. Soon they will be over my roof, over my head, clashing and fusing, air pressure rising and falling, two fronts colliding directly above me, wall against menacing wall—*is predicted with the arrival of a new mass of cold air, but those in the south might experience snowfall until Thursday evening*—the falling end emerges victorious, it will be an early winter. What else is there to do aside from harvest basil and thyme?—*the lowlands can expect weak to mild winds from the east to* —northeast, I was there already. I will make some nice blends this year, blend number three will be especially delectable, épice riche—*otherwise quite pleasant*—pleasant, yes I know that. Quite pleasant overall. "Overall," that is especially important, as it allows the pleasantness to spread out, to expand—*gradual decline*—"gradual" is not an adjective—*but for the meantime, it will remain*—here comes the fog line again!—*fog line will remain at 800 meters, the air pressure in northern Europe*—if the fog line were to rise just a little, if the white wall, the cloud, were to float slightly upward, it would reach me—*expect that the disturbance will shift from the west in a southerly to southeasterly direction*—until it is over my house—*but those in the south might experience continued*—snowfall—snow—*until Thursday evening*—enough.

So snow, then. That's alright with me. The arrival of cold air. An advancing fog line, whose mass engulfs me, displaced by circular wind patterns—I have made my peace with the happenings up above, from here there is nothing one can do about them—I will welcome whatever comes my way. Lying, loosely floating between a mild draft from below, shifting gusts from the sides, and precipitation from above—I surrender myself happily, the middle is a good place to be.

Place to be? Where am I, then? Where? Here—nowhere. Nowhere, the only place where I can breathe, free, liberated from everything, pressured by nothing except the weather. No conversations to hold, no assignments to complete, no judgment to render, no guilt to bear, no skill to master, save from my miniscule contribution to the field of gastronomy, no god to pray to—but how lovely it would have been to summon more rain from the heavens now and again—no path to tread, except the one running through the gardens; other than this, there is nothing, nothing—I allow myself be carried along until I cease to be.

Fog line. Snow line, snowfall: I see myself at the road leading up to the pass. It is iced over, a sharp wind from the east or the northeast swirls about or sweeps over hillsides and cornices and plains, chasing billows of snow and ice crystals into the air, a whistling cloud that steals the breath and chokes the voice; not a shape to be seen, save for the stakes protruding from the ground next to the shoulder, demarcating the road's edge, or rather what was road during the summer, and what will, next summer, be road once again. A sign appears on the right, a warning sign, but there is nothing on it, the surface has been pelted with snow, white like everything else, the horizon is nowhere to be found—

—when was that? It was already spring by then. I drove, drove for the sake of driving, up to the pass—I just wanted to go up, I had no goal other than to go up. The road had been cleared,

sharply cut snow on both sides, but new snow had fallen, block-
ing the pass once again. Travel at your own risk.

But I continue on anyway, I love doing things at my own
risk. There is fog everywhere, white and gray-white, no outlines
are visible, no objects other than the snowdrifts and a few pine
trees behind a cloud of gray mist, no shadows, and no sun to
cast them, earth and sky and mountain and road run together
into one, and soon even the snow itself begins to float and dance;
thrown into chaos by the weaving curves, it spins and ricochets
like bowling pins struck by the explosive power of a well-aimed
ball. As I continue upward, a steady stream of snow spewing
from under my chained tires, I resolve to let my memories be
my guide, but the closer I come to them, the more they dwindle,
floating diffusely in front of me like an ignis fatuus, laughing
at me as they fade into the darkness, perhaps I have already
been led astray—and suddenly another presence enters my gaze:
death, he's been waiting here, waiting upon this blank page for
the perfect moment to make an entrance, as a cloud of mist, the
Ace of Spades, the Boogie Man, the tarot player, the engraver,
the child hunter, Halunke, the accomplice whom nobody finds
out. He knows the various effects his presence can have—we
must grant him that.

And it is not long before my car, overpowered by the relentless onslaught of snow, grinds to a halt as well. Milling the
white powder beneath them to hard, packed sheets of ice, the
chain-bound tires frantically spin and clatter, like a machine
out of control. The motor, its final efforts met with unmoving
resistance, wails in fury as bursts of ice crystals pelt the side
windows. One last push on the gas, one last anguished yelp, and
it dies, and then nothing but silence; the world, and everything
in it, everything I have ever known, every object I have ever
touched, and every sight I have ever seen, has turned away from
me. It's over.

But in the end I did walk away from this, if you will pardon the slight inaccuracy of my expression. Ever so gradually, with a determined, resolute slowness, without me so much as shifting my weight in my seat, the car begins to turn, as if a vertical axle has risen from the ground and taken hold of the vehicle's underbelly, rotating it with the leisurely, but measured precision of a dealership display stand. Now situated diagonally across the road, the car starts to slide backward, until the rear bumper collides abruptly with another wall of snow a few meters away, causing the vehicle to bounce slightly before continuing its zigzag-like descent. The front bumper grinds against piled snow and I turn the steering wheel, determined not to allow this merciful coincidence to go to waste. I set a course down the mountain and try to maintain a controlled slide; a slight turn causes the fender to scrape up against the wall of snow on my right, creating a groove that grows deeper and deeper until suddenly there is something hard, grating, a wall of metal. As the snow begins to fall away, I am gradually able to see what I've uncovered: another car.

A 1952 Chevrolet limousine in light blue. And inside the window, paralyzed, suffocated, frozen, hardened, likely since the previous autumn, no jacket, panama hat strung around his neck, a handkerchief stuffed between his shirt and jacket collar, in a gray-blue gabardine suit and loosened yellow tie, hands crossed over the steering wheel, sat the great evangelist himself, Mr. Wesley B. Prosniczer. His mouth, which housed an unusually white set of teeth, formed a loud, but now long since faded A, the A of a hymn to be sure. His eyes were closed, as if in his last moments he had wanted to see nothing, applying the full power of his fervent concentration instead to the singing of the word and the realization of its meaning. Looking in through the window at him, I did not detect an aura of wellness or peace in the stiff body, exposed for all souls to see, a man of such trivial belief, for even if freezing, on account of its preservative effect, could be considered a rather wonderful form of death compared

to its disfiguring alternatives, the premature immortalization of
Prosniczer's youthful features had likely come as an unwelcome
surprise. But I won't think about that right now—

—perhaps I'll try to sleep. What was that beautiful name again?
Tynset.

It's actually not so beautiful, and there are certainly finer,
more harmonious names. And there are probably—of course
I cannot be sure—there are probably more beautiful places in
Norway than this Tynset, an insignificant stop on a similarly
insignificant branch line between Hamar and Støren, a gray
town with a view of gray mountains, barren mountains. But
nonetheless, my thoughts have chosen this place, and they continue to circle it. Earlier, they were more rambling, but not for
some time now; they used to glide over dozens of wondrous
names on the map—not to mention through the constellations
in the sky; these were glorious journeys, soaring to immeasurable
heights, but here

here they have come upon a roadblock. Now, perhaps it was
a long time coming, yes, that it was: a long time coming, and
when I think back, I am surprised it didn't happen sooner, now
that I am no longer planning an escape, now that the horrific
is losing its horror.

I pick up my notepad from its place on the night table and write
in block letters, bolt upright, with painfully straight horizontal
crossbars, save for the conspicuous diagonal of the Y: TYNSET.
It stands there on the page like barren plots in a snowy garden—
no, that's not right, it stands there like a symbol on the wall, as
if it had written itself. But what does it mean?

As it stands there, it begins to grow, to take on meaning, and
I begin to decorate it, adding a few small ornaments around the
letters; true, they detract somewhat from the name's growing
pathos, but they also serve to temper its harsh severity.

What does it mean? Nothing. I lay the notepad back down

onto the night table, atop the mound of newspapers, magazines, and the telephone book, one of many telephone books, actually, which I still read through now and again when, while daydreaming, I find myself on the verge of surrendering to the illusion that this world is unpopulated.

There was, by the way, a time when I tried to write a telephone book myself, as an exercise. I began with A, but I couldn't think of anything—the pressure of the first letter hindered any attempt to achieve unity in a sea of information. There were too many parameters. I then turned to my card file in an attempt to break free from my former dependence on letters, engaging instead in a game of constantly multiplying possibilities. But this too I abandoned quickly, it was a senseless endeavor: at no point does one stray farther from the trail of life than when trying to replicate it. It was like trying to make a footprint with my hand. And even I, on several occasions, made the mistake of reckoning without my host, the host of us all, who stood behind me and sneered silently over my shoulder, his bony finger pointing out each inconsistency, each tiny improbability, which, try as I might, I could not resolve. I could plainly see that something did not fit, but illumination evaded me, until I was forced to compare my work with the official telephone book in order to locate the error—which was always quite small, hardly detectable by the naked eye—that was responsible for marring the unity of the image. No, that's not the right word, it's too weak: the image wasn't marred, it was destroyed, or better yet, exterminated, yes, that's the word I wanted: exterminated. For things that are said or read or written or thought or printed or preached, it's never a question of good or bad. It's a question of wrong or right, and that goes for my telephone book as well: it was wrong.

An example: I was once working on a certain Dr. Hanskarl Fuhrich, who I had decided was a graphologist residing at 24 Lichtenbergallee, admittedly a rather sophisticated address for

somebody who has dedicated his life to such a far-flung branch
of science, the validity of which, even today, is quite hotly con-
tested. But even still, the combination seemed real to me, I think
on account of its pleasing sound. I later discovered him in the
official telephone book: a man with precisely this name and
very same profession I had assigned to him. The only thing is he
didn't live at 24 Lichtenbergallee, but instead at 9a Judengasse—
and just like that, a legally certified expert, a specialist of great
repute, sank down to a lower class, becoming a dubious fringe
scientist with a reputation a mere step above that of an astrol-
ogist, a hack with falsified degrees who, even on a street like
Judengasse, gave the neighborhood a bad name.

In fact, pretty much everything turned out to be dingier and
more lackluster than my draft had presented it, despite my
deluded belief that I had succeeded in capturing the tired tedium
of this structured system. When I tried to correct my error,
to pave a more modest path and populate it with a few similarly modest people—I never thought in terms of families, the
telephone book does not list families, which is without doubt
one of its most fatal flaws—I would, in accordance with my
intentions, end up with entries such as Adolf G. Schmöldes,
Product Representative, 78 Schlachthofgasse (personally, I find
the address somewhat of a stretch, its convolutedness too intentional), where last name, profession, number, and this time even
the street address would correspond perfectly to a living person, only the first name was not actually Adolf G., but Götz
Friedrich. Another correction from my omnipresent editor, and
this time for an entirely unexpected reason: I had not in any
way accounted for parents who, in an attempt to ameliorate the
dissonance of inherited letters—whose presence they themselves
have suffered for a lifetime—endow their children with a pithy,
noble-sounding first name; in essence, it was quite an under-
standable, if not futile, attempt to even the playing field for a
disadvantaged son, who, in the end, probably wouldn't manage

to get out of Schlachthofgasse anyway, whiling away his life at some company down the street, selling knife sharpeners or cleaning products or miscellaneous, time-saving kitchen gadgets. It's places like this where the telephone book is able to reflect the unspoken, where we are afforded an abrupt, fleeting glimpse into a world of repressed, silent tragedy.

Götz Friedrich—didn't I know somebody with that name? Yes, I did, he was a schoolmate of mine and he was always riding a motorcycle, the only trait of his I still remember. He was in an accident once, but tenaciously maintained his hold on life. His passenger, however, another classmate, whose name I have forgotten, was not so fortunate.

A name like that sticks, so much so, in fact, that it has a distinct influence on one's perception of its carrier, who is at first innocent, undeserving of the premature judgments, but who soon begins to grow into them, like he grows into everything—he grows into his schema like he grows into his guilt. It's a name that precedes the child, like hubris precedes a fall, but it is not just the parents—whichever of them it was who could not conceive of naming the child anything else—upon whom it reflects, but its carrier as well, who, as the years go by, becomes inseparable from the name, becomes its flesh and blood; the name soon embodies itself in him, becomes a symbol, a banner that ripples in the breath of every person who speaks to him and who utters the name aloud, and at other times a flag, billowing in the wind of entitlement, a swell of presumptuous justification. Götz Friedrich, Giselher, Armgard: names like these don't just appear out of nowhere. These are inherited titles, drunk with the mother's milk and nourished, growing, as they were predestined to do, until they become one with their owner and their owner one with them: great, demanding, threatening. True, we are all free to change our names later in life. Ronald Fleming, for example, used to be called Karl Mädler. He had hoped that this change would help rid him of a certain flaw he had discovered in himself, but he failed to notice that the new name didn't fit him. As a result he only succeeded in drawing more attention to the weakness he had been trying to disguise in the first place, namely, the desire to be somebody he was not and would never become. For you see, the person he desired to be, Ronald Fleming, would never have even considered changing his name.

It is stupid to call yourself something other than your name, it's about as stupid as cosmetic surgery. For example . . .

. . . for example, Doris Wiener, who had an operation to even out her nose and make it smaller. Afterwards, it was impossible to ignore the pre-operative blemish that shone through from behind the manipulated beauty of her post-operative face. The flaw was not physically noticeable, of course, but was quite apparent in the soul of the beautified woman, in her eyes and her guilty gaze, which always looked past you in a hopeless search for an object to cling to. It was the gaze of uprootedness, of somebody who had abandoned the imperfection endowed to her by real circumstances. And because of this—yes, I remember now—because of this, it was impossible for the man who married her ever to understand her completely, for the small part of her that was sawn—or rather, filed—off of her had not taken a correspondingly small piece of her identity with it. In fact, it had added something: a nice, rounded dent, and a feeling of loss. Of course, I don't know whether her husband ever became aware of what was missing, if he—

if he even had time to find out. Both of them went out early, you see. Went out, that's what you call it. They went out in a gas chamber—installed by a company named Föttle & Geiser, I have an unfailing memory of company names—and he, whose name was Bloch, by the way, he was, if I remember correctly, the only person I have ever known who literally dug his own grave, under the watch of Kabasta, who then led him up to the edge and shot him in the back of the head with his right hand, his huge, red and yellow right hand.

The Roosters of Attica: to hear them crowing, I climbed up to the Acropolis one evening, just before closing time, and hid behind one of the giant Doric columns as the night guards made their final pass through the temple and across the broad, stony grounds. As they moved, I moved with them, pressed against the column's hollow grooves like a gear cog, remaining obscured from view while awaiting the opportune moment to sneak inside. I knew I had a long night ahead of me, but I was not scared. Even then I was not much of a sleeper: all of my nights were long.

Early the next morning, before daybreak, at the moment when the sun had betrayed the first fleeting hint of its presence, a sensation you feel first in your bones, and then on your skin like a frosty breath, as the humming and the buzzing of the night grows quicker and more volatile, at this moment I positioned myself on the eastern wall, where an oriel window had been installed for tourists wishing to take photographs, cupped my hands in front of my mouth, and screamed as loud as I could: *Kikeriki!*

Silence. For a moment, it was completely silent, more silent, even, than it had been earlier, as if my cry had stolen the air from the sounds of the night, and robbed them of their purpose. In this moment, I felt shame, shame for the act of foolishness I had just committed. For at this hour, in this silence, at this place, where the breath of the gods—and the crooks and villains beneath them—had not yet dissipated, even the smallest, most insignificant act of foolishness lingers in the air, a representative of all foolish acts. This was followed by a brief moment of illumination, but I didn't reach for it and instead let it pass by and disappear again, reabsorbed into the air. And then, as I waited for an answer, or even an echo, to my call, something happened: not far off from where I was standing, below the wall, in the corner of what in the old city must have been a backyard, there was a noise, a sluggish scratching against metal and wood, the sleepy fluttering of wings. My call had awakened an old, worn-out rooster, who, now, in a hoarse, raspy voice that betrayed its years of use, answered me. His *kikeriki* was not very clearly articulated, too much *i* and not enough *k,* but it served to break the silence. The call sounded only once, but now I knew that another being was awake, a connection had been established— true, it was just a silly rooster, but these are the hours when one is thankful for any kind of contact.

I repeated my cry, and this time the backyard rooster answered immediately: he was prepared; he had been waiting. I did not cry back. But now the rooster was fully awake, expectant, I heard him flutter his wings and scratch against a hollow piece of metal—he had tipped over a box. Suddenly, in a rather prosaic way, the night seemed alive. I heard him cry again, this time in disappointed expectation. And somewhere, farther away this time, but still quite close, a second rooster answered, a younger one—I could hear the blossom of youth in the brassy tenor of his voice. He crowed once, and then was silent again: the game had gotten off to a rather hesitant start. I waited for a moment longer, but before the last echo had died away, I cupped my hands once again and cried *kikeriki,* to spur on the action, a cue for the players to begin the concert. This time, it was the young rooster who answered first, farther in the distance than before, but still close enough, and then, barely detectable above the blaring of his partner, the old backyard rooster mustered a response, his voice drawing nearer and nearer to failure.

At this point I didn't need to cry anymore, for the young rooster was now wide awake. In the physicality and passion of his voice I heard the desperate desire to arouse. And no sooner had he crowed again than yet another voice entered. The third rooster's call was deep and droning, but also rather far away,

perhaps at the foot of Hymettus, or in that direction at least, and
with him crowed yet another, this time from down in the old
city, the bold tone of a warrior. He was a neighbor to the backyard rooster that I had first encountered, and I wondered why he
hadn't crowed earlier. The backyard rooster was now silent—he
had sung with all his might but eventually had been forced to
surrender, unable to withstand the ever-increasing intensity of
the exchange around him, this heraldic tournament of voices,
volleying back and forth between a brassy tenor, a deep droner,
and a dauntless warrior. And then a fourth, a trumpeter, farther
away still than any of the others, from the flatlands that stretch
toward Cape Sounion, his voice trailed off in the breeze. There
followed a pause, a surprised pause, as if the initial group of
three had not expected another participant, and then another
wave of sound, four distinct notes fired off in quick succession,
one after the other, and then again, but in a different order this
time, as if the first attempt had not been satisfactory; a fifth
from the south, and a sixth from the west, both far away, and
a seventh, closer again, close enough that I could hear an echo.
As the reverberations grew weaker, the others started in again,
the droner, the trumpeter, the warrior, and the brassy tenor, the
fifth from the south and the sixth from the west, and then the
seventh again, and then the echo, but this time it did not die—
the others did not let it; and then there were new voices, near
and far, high and low, hoarse and clear, new tenors, new trum-
peters, new warriors, droners, fanfares, castrati. There were so
many now that it was impossible to hear the individuals—they
were coming from all directions, and the concert was spreading
like wildfire, racing through the mountains, its echoes bouncing
from rock faces, across the flatlands and into the valleys, into
regions so far away that they were barely audible to me and the
roosters in my vicinity, who were quickly becoming hoarse. As
voices died out, new ones took their place, broadening, intensifying, multiplying, until all pitches and all registers of the
male voice, from the deepest bass to the highest falsetto, were

being sounded at once. And so it spread, this Attic concert, through the surrounding land, in every direction. It was like a net that constantly grew wider as its holes became smaller and smaller—newly awakened voices continued to join in, calling and listening and calling again, but no one heard the entirety; the roosters could only hear and respond to what was directly around them, in their local radius, the length and location of which varied for each individual. The net of crowing had now turned into a carpet, whose tassels continued to expand, thicken, and weave together as the concert spread in all directions. Only upon reaching the ocean did it stop: the roosters on the coast directed their calls inland, cutting their circles of influence in half, and those on peninsulas and spits aimed inward as well, covering only a small sector of land, while the rest of their calls were swallowed by the waves. And far away, the rooster of Cape Sounion turned his back to the land and called out over the water. Perhaps he was heard by an early morning fisherman, who would not have heard just the single voice, but an entire, jagged coastline full of crowing, near and far, shooting out to sea and bouncing back to land again, echoing all the way to Athens, and then farther still, breaking off in all directions, and then back again, and eventually returning to me, the originator, the source. Standing atop the hill, I reign in silence over the crowing birds below me, Prince of the Roosters, King of the Roosters of Attica, presiding over the great concert and asking myself how it will come to an end.

But end it did, it died. The night became thinner, more thread-bare, and here and there a call began to fade, while others died off entirely; more and more voices fell out of the chorus, and in the distance, islands of quiet began to surface amidst the waves of sound, the night was dissolving, losing itself, getting lighter and lighter as the new day awakened, and with it, the hens. For some of the roosters, this simply meant a distraction, a cue to begin a day's work of copulation. And with that they were gone, their loneliness vanquished, as if they had never been there in the first place. Islands of sound in a sea of quiet. And finally, it was back to a few, one close by and two farther away, who, undefeated, undefeatable, continued to crow, yearning in vain for the night to return, for the great concert to resume. But as the daylight grew brighter, even they recognized the futility of reassembling the masculine brotherhood of the night. They crowed once more and were silent. It was quiet again, brighter and cold, the cold emptiness before the heat rises, and then it began, timidly at first, but then faster, unstoppable: the clattering, chattering, and rumbling of an Athenian morning. The nighttime concert was now a thing of the past, and as I left my post on the wall to hide from the morning guards, I felt the memory slip away as its object became more distant. And it was not until much, much later that I would be able to evoke it again.

During a night like this, I would never want to sleep. But, as I have told myself before, a real sleeper cannot be kept awake by any noise, no matter what its nature. The Duke of Wellington, for example, slept through the Battle of Bar-le-Duc, one of his most decisive victories, and when he awoke the next morning around ten o'clock and demanded his chocolate, his generals informed him that he had won. That's what I call a sleeper, a talented sleeper.

Where was I? Roosters and sleepers. What sleepers? No, I was talking about Doris Wiener and Bloch—no, no, I was talking about names, names and noses.

Names and noses—you can't simply cut away a flaw, or wash it from your face. Flaws never leave because they are never forgotten. In fact, it's only through the first attempt at eradication that the flaw gains real significance. People don't change, and this goes just as much for their noses as it does for their names and secret desires. Take me, for example: I bear a name with an embarrassing undertone, originating in some faraway, pre-historic depth, a foggy darkness I have always been afraid to look into. To be sure, I could give myself the most glorious name possible; I could rub against the walls of distant cities, let the winds of remote regions blow through me, until, bearded and browned, I laugh a laugh that nobody recognizes; I could pile on nicknames in an attempt to suffocate the real one, attach syllables and vowels, taken from southern or northern regions; but even then I would not be rid of it, it would not be erased. But even if I did succeed, my outer self would go with it, clinging to the lie like Hercules's skin to the Nessus robe, making visible my inner self, where everyone, regardless of whether or not they knew my name beforehand, or if they even cared, would see it, carved into my flesh and blood: there it stands, there it is.

Eleven o'clock.

Now—now I am growing old, it's beginning. It's always now, always at this hour, between eleven and twelve, when aging takes place, the nightly ritual—and me its obedient victim. For the other twenty-three hours of the day, it remains still, like the clock at a train station: for almost an entire minute, the hand is frozen in place, until suddenly, in the final fraction of a second, it leaps forward to the next position. And so I leap as well, as the final traces of the day vanish, leap to the next day, older now by this leap, older by this day—it's not so much of a leap, though. It's more of a slip.

I am growing older, I can feel it as I lie here. The indentation in my mattress grows deeper and deeper as the years go by—while the years themselves seem to get shorter—and my bed grows softer. A bolster, as they used to call it. Bolster, that's an odd word. But in reality, I'm sure nobody ever said it. Reality—?

I lie there, sinking deeper, always a little deeper, into the bed, as if my back were being drawn downward toward the center of the earth. Sinking—through each and every layer, through my bed, the floor, the ground, through granite and gneiss and malm and dogger, farther down, backward, softly—softly, deeper and deeper, and above me, I see everything coming back together, closing, as if I had never even been there. If I am no more, then I will never have been.

I feel—

—I feel a humming, a flow, a gentle current, a gradual disappearance, under my skin I feel myself getting older. But my skin is getting older as well. And my breath. Old breath! Not to mention my thoughts—if I can really refer to what I think as thoughts, these splinters, these fragments, dislodged yearnings, the object of which I can no longer remember or am in the process of forgetting at this moment. My memory is giving out, everything is fading, turning away from me, people, events, friendships, love affairs—and it is only the senselessness that remains, that swims above me—

and yet: there are still moments, short interruptions, caesuras, along the way, decelerations, moments where foreignness makes sense: me here, the deceptive beauty of the world there—and then it's gone again—

—a late autumn day, October, but an October that is turning Novembery as the mist rolls in, high above me; all around, the gulls are screaming through the foggy air, a west wind is blowing, a sea wind, still mild, but with a cold, wintry core. There is white, too, a white steamboat with white smokestacks bumps up against the tires hanging down from the edge of the dock: "Firestone."— "Firestone"—the cables grate against the bollard, groaning as if they're about to snap, but they don't. They just get raw and stringy as they scrape the bollard bare. But one day they will snap, everything will snap. A line of rust creeps across the white hull, downward from the anchor pocket, the chains roll, loading cranes, trolleys—and I—I see the ship under my feet, and I see the ship next to me, I am standing on the dock and I am standing on the ship, a rocking deck beneath my feet, or solid, stone ground, I am in the picture, I am not in the picture, I am looking at myself from the outside, I am alone, we are there together—

together?—but with whom?

A female voice calls out, but even though its owner is standing right next to me, her words are blown away by the wind, I see them disappear, dissolve—the wind blows through her hair, it is blonde or black, the seagulls are light gray, the ship is white with a red line of rust, the sky is gray—

the sky is gray—yes, it is this last banality that makes it all disappear: gray autumn sky. There was a time when the sky was blue, but the blue is now washed out, tattered, worn out by people like me, and now the sky is gray. I set the picture aside, I am here again, in this great big bed, my winter bed; I return to the passage of time: it is between eleven and twelve now. After meeting my nightly aging quota, I take the thin threads into my hands once again and begin weaving a rope, a rope that will pull me forward, forward, downward, away, where the path grows smaller, always smaller, where the possibilities wilt and fall away—possibilities?

—The red wine bottle is empty. I should get a new one from the kitchen. Later, later—I should—

—I should go to Tynset. That would really be something, wouldn't it? To leave the house after all these years, to push off and swim into the unknown, or the no-longer-known. That would be my destination, the only possible, the only conceivable one. But slowly—slowly would I draw near, no hurry. I would look around, act like I have no goal, and sometimes I would even believe myself, linger in peace at various stations as if each of them were the endpoint. No, not that, I should stop deceiving myself on this, my last journey. I could never forget my destination, not Tynset. But to savor the transitions, enjoy what there is to enjoy, the slow changes, the first appearance of unfamiliar fields, foreign waterways, announcements of lower latitude, promises of the north, the first breath of cool air, kites, magpies—and slowly learning what awaits me in Tynset, and what doesn't.

Yes, I will go there. There is now only the matter of the cities, the elongated fortifications, labyrinthine flight traps, barely penetrable, interlocking, stitched together in an eternal state of ruthless competition—I should avoid these if possible. By traveling there, even in passing, I would become a witness to their growth, I would see them as they expand, spilling over onto untouched fields, consuming mountains of rubble only to spew them out again someplace else, becoming so giant as to engulf small villages, lap up gardens, flatten the land around them in order to plant seeds that will soon grow into satellite towns, burrowing downward only to spring from the ground yet again, expanding in all directions, killing off the earth in all seven dimensions, unpredictable—no, not unpredictable, just poorly predicted—and they will flourish, turning to metastases overnight, invisible yesterday, and not even detectable the day before, but a tumor today, and tomorrow the blackened center of decaying tissue, chains of small concrete ulcers, one just like the other, and each surrounded by planted, fenced-in waste. They crop up on eroded hillsides, or alongside access roads, streets form quadratic nets around the colonies of concrete ulcers, and soon there are suburbs, which turn to cities, and then metropolises, ready to spawn a new strain of satellites, where nobody knows the way, even those who grew up there. Eventually these cities will turn to ruins, and after centuries, in the predictable but unpredicted future, there will be deserts once again—

—much in the same way that the Nabataean kingdom turned back to desert, to the same desert from which it arose, a city from the desert, and me standing at its periphery, breathing in the sand, in the singeing midday heat, desert to my back, on both sides of me, desert behind the yellow, crumbling walls, and desert far ahead of me, visible through the stone archway in the city's center, and all of it under a yellowy gray, murderous sky—there was death here, death in the desert, the death of many, of everything I have experienced my entire life long, a death that hammers home what life means: delusion and deception and humiliation. One of the many deaths I was prepared to die, and perhaps have died already.

I have died many times, but these days I don't do it as often. Eventually, it will have to be the last time. But I'm putting that off for now, none of the deaths I have encountered thus far have been particularly convincing, and I never know whether a better one is on its way. I will only live once, which makes life somewhat of an experiment, but I die often, for there are a range of different possibilities for the final analysis and conclusion. Possibilities: I don't mean for me, but instead for the entity that brought me to life, that watches me and waits with bated breath to see which death I eventually choose.

Now, however, I know that the next death will be the last one. It will be in a house, encased in wood, omnipresent; it has selected me, I am its charge, and nobody else may approach, for it has already proclaimed: this one belongs to me.

I am the little boy in that story, the one who cries "Wolf!" The thing is, the story was told incorrectly: the boy expected the wolf every time, awaited him, and every time he suffered death by decapitation, although it scared him less and less with each attack, and not once did he expect that somebody would come to his aid.

A yellow-gray sky, and far in the distance, on the other side of the arch, and visible through it, far, far away in the desert, a black point appears and begins to grow, becoming blacker, thicker, thicker still, and longer—

as I stand there before the kingdom of the Nabatea—

I was not alone—but who was it? Who was with me?

—it is hot, I can see the heat shimmering between me and the
heavens, thick, viscous, mercurial; it burns within me, and as I
stand there I see no one, just this point on the horizon, growing blacker, longer, taller; it's approaching, it's walking, coming
toward the archway, toward me. Now it has reached the arch, it
comes through, but the arch is far away; between it and me there
lies a giant swath of empty space, city, desert; the growing point
crosses the space, but is still nowhere close to me, this figure,
growing larger and longer, continually approaching—is it death?

But why now? Why here, at this hour, when I cannot protect myself from these images, when I would be delivered to
him at his most repulsive, his most ridiculous? Why should he
appear to me here, so slow, so dignified, in the middle of such a
well-chosen, well-measured frame? Why like this, and not as a
monster, to me, who has scorned him so harshly and—yes, it's
futile, I'm aware—denied him so vehemently? Were I to atone
for all of my blasphemies, I would need to live again, but living
again is not something I wish to do. No, not that.

But it isn't him, it isn't death—as the figure comes closer,
ambling over to me, I can see that it is not dressed in black,
but instead in white, with a white headscarf. The scarf does not
billow, for there is no wind, everything is still.

That was her. But who was she? What color was her hair, her
skin? What did her voice sound like? Perhaps I loved her,
whoever she was—after all, one does not often find oneself in
the desert, in a dead city, with somebody who doesn't mean
anything.

She came up next to me, put her arm around my shoulder,
and I was redeemed. It was not death after all, just an illusion;

and now my vision is clear again, the city is empty, the archway
open, which means that it is once again possible for him to

appear as a monster, something repulsive or something ridiculous, and that I could be right after all about my last breath
being in the form of a laugh, mocking the ridiculousness of
death, that I won't allow myself to be frightened, that I will
remain the victor. And even if in my entire life, in this tightly
woven chain of inanity, even if I had never in my life wanted to
be right—and believe me, it is rather a burden to be right all of
the time, just once I would have enjoyed being wrong—I very
much want to be right about this, this and then never again.
Despite the fact that I would have no time to enjoy my triumph,
to celebrate my victory—if you can really call being definitively
right a victory. Yes, I think you can. In fact, if you look at it the
right way, it is the only real victory one can have.

There—there it is again, the point, it is approaching again from
the other side of the archway, floating closer and closer, floating
through it now, but this time the black remains black, cloaked,
masked, like one of the Parcae, a choirmaster who silently begins
a Lamento, but without a chorus to join him. There it is again,
striding toward me through the heat of a desert afternoon, noise-
less, across the vast yellow terrain, black—it reminds me—what
does it remind me of?—it reminds me of nothing, that's it, nothing. I have never seen anything like this—
      Now it is no longer striding, but floating above the ground,
floating toward me, no, swinging, no, definitely not that, it's
fluttering, like a bat, lurching through the air like a black leaf-
let, spreading the message of the Kaiser's death through all the
lands—it must have been carried here by the wind, although
here it is of no interest to anybody. It is death, yes, this time it's
really death, fluttering, as if, even at his ridiculous, unspeakable age, he had not yet managed to fly, not even that. That is
ridiculous, laughable really—and I am laughing—laughing—

Have I slept? Only a couple of minutes. Did I dream? No, I
didn't dream, as far as I know. Where was I before? In Nabatea.

Everywhere. Nowhere. On a weary search. Resigned to everything. Prepared, braced for anything.

Tynset. Didn't I want to do some research about Tynset? Yes,
that was it. That's what I wanted to do. Trace the paths, travel
the streets, find lodging, ask a guide, open a map—

I stand up and put on my slippers. It is cold, and I'm wearing a
nightshirt, white, long, rather ridiculous looking—but it's only
a feigned ridiculousness; I feel good, dignified in my linen cloak,
which is similar to the cloak I will don when I confront death
for the last time; it makes no concessions to the demands of
daylight or life; it scorns pajamas, the fearful accessory of the
well-dressed gentleman, and the fly of the combat-ready cavalier,
cut to confront nocturnal adversaries with confidence and ease.

Don't forget the bottle. I wanted to get a new one from the
kitchen. I take the flashlight and pass through the empty room,
where there is nothing—save for the whispered creaking of the
wood and the quiet bubbling of the fountain outside—that I
cannot hear from my bedroom as well.

The fountain is located in the garden, under an overgrown wall.
It ripples, it has always rippled, and will continue to ripple until
the end of all rippling, rippling into eternity. During the day it
is drowned out, but at night, it drowns out the night—no, not
that, rather, it is one of the many voices that make up the night's
choir. The water flows through the summer and winter, it flows
and flows. In the winter, errant drops burst against the walls
and form misshapen ice sculptures around the main stream,
dampening the fountain's noise and making it sound as if it
were coming from a grotto. And sometimes, summer or winter,
but only sometimes, the stream of water stops for a fraction of
a second, the water spits and sputters, chokes, forming short
phrases in Morse code, something invisible flits past, some other
incarnation of death, with his parlor tricks, remaining on the

periphery and reminding everybody, not anybody in particular, but everybody who cares to lend an ear, in a very general and—it seems to me—not altogether unfriendly manner, that he is even master of the dancing water, when he wants to be.

But this death is not my death either, mine is not out there at the fountain, nor is it up on the snowy pass or in the city in the desert. Mine is in the house, perhaps somewhere by the drying herbs, or even here in this empty room. He is trying to retain a sense of pride, and we must grant him that. He turns up here now and again, visible, but discrete—he does not wish to disturb; he stands there as if by chance, behind drawn curtains in the early evening hours or in the middle of a heavy afternoon, disappears, and then, unexpectedly, returns; his visit is briefer this time, but more insistent, his presence is clearer, more persistent; he follows me with a loose, flexible gait—maybe he's practicing his walk; he follows me into the library and from there into the other rooms, or even goes ahead of me and then turns around as if looking for somebody else. He loses himself in the house's twists and turns, or he comes with me, making my search for some forgotten, unused object more difficult, but abruptly forcing me, when I have found it, to remember the time of its last use, and then he disappears again, and then he is back, and I see his false smile, he seems to be asking for clemency of some kind, for he is, after all, merely the servant of a higher power. Sometimes he sneers—yes, the sneer of death is a rather banal image, but he does sneer, and he is banal—he sneers at my humiliation upon realizing the superfluousness of some of the items that have come into my possession over the years, that I have picked up out of the dust somewhere, objects that have long since been retired from service—he stands next to me, and suddenly something falls from my hand, shattering on the floor, or perhaps it fell from the shelf for no reason at all; he is there, and I am there, I stand there like little Kai with a splinter in my eye, and suddenly the beautiful becomes questionable, and the questionable absurd, and the absurd even more absurd than before, yes, worthless. Yesterday it had belonged, it had a place, no matter how insignificant, but today it is fossilized and covered in dust, intolerable. This is how all things around me lose their worth.

No, not all things. Spread about the room, standing, lying, and hanging, are certain objects that I acquired not for the sake of possession, so to speak, but for the mysteries enshrouding them—no, yet again I am not expressing myself correctly: these objects are not shrouded in mystery. It is more that these objects were witnesses to mysteries of the past, silent material, without the promise of revelation, discrete protectors of their secrets; my two beds, for example, or the painting I hung in the northern light of one of the upstairs rooms.

The painting to which I am referring is in landscape dimensions, with a heavy gold-plated frame. The oil paint on the old, stiff canvas, probably applied one hundred and fifty years ago, is brittle, cracked, and dull, darkened, black even, to the point where it's impossible to draw even the slightest conclusion about what it once portrayed. On the bottom left it is signed: Jean Gaspard Muller. The signature is not darkened, which means there are two possibilities: either the signature was added later—but that is unlikely. After all, who would sign a darkening, or already black, painting other than the painter?—or the painting was always black; one hundred fifty years ago, a man named Muller painted a black painting. Jean Gaspard. Gaspard de la nuit—

I am in the library and I turn on a light, illuminating the walls of books. Yes, walls of books, that is the right description. Where in these rows and piles can I find something about Tynset? They've been out of order for years now, ever since I pulled in the anchor, ever since the beginning of my slow, at first not even noticeable departure from the firm clarity of organization into the horizonless fog of indecision.

I peruse the sections with telephone books and railway time-tables, which I have collected for a long time, and which I am still collecting, even if my current efforts lack their former rigor, or the pleasure of acquisition. These days, it's much more a matter of trusting coincidence. I look where I believe the guide-books—of which I have a few—to be, but I find none, they must be somewhere else. Other items have collected here—I quickly determine that this has become the miscellaneous section, the contribution section. This is where I put everything that has ever been sent to me, the well-intentioned gifts, innocent print on tolerant paper, specimens of fallacy, of false interpretation, and false assessment of what moves me, and what has ever moved me.

Mieses/van der Raalte: *The 100 Most Beautiful Chess Matches in the World.*

Vangatesha Narayana Sharma: *The Book of the Seven Truths,* with a foreword by Carl Gustav Jung.

A guide to Uhland's operas and operettas.

Pönsgen-Bscherer: *An Overview of Social Hygiene.*

The Book of the Seven Truths again. I remember that I used to own multiple copies of this book. Every year for my birthday I would receive it from the same person: a forgetful friend of my mother's, who was hopelessly obsessed with Eastern philosophy, until one day she joined a nationalist movement and put a demonstrative end to her tenacious gift-giving. I can no longer remember her name. Moving on:

Polycarp Schmiehelt S. J.: *Christianity and the Atom Bomb.*

Is Germany Still a Problem? A Symposium, edited by Gerhard Schürenberg and Walter Maria Menzel.

Prof. Dr. Karl Wilhelm Herrenacker: *Who Was Parsifal's Wife, and Lohengrin's Mother?* Topics in German Mythology, vol. 97.

A table of logarithms.

"What Remains?" On the Situation of Today's Society, by Theodor Gesenius-Everding.

Hans-Gert Oppelt: *The Border,* a novel.

A photo collection: *The Beauty of Kochertal.*

Odoard Smyrrka: *Hvlosved Amsjeda Hamleta gorevle?*

How did this book get here? I haven't read it—I don't even understand the language. Perhaps it was given to me by somebody who thought I did?

I remove the volume from its place on the shelf. A page from a letter falls out. It reads:

"dressed as a Biedermeier couple, the cousins ad-libbed a performance of a song composed by our great-grandfather, von Borsig. He had written this duet originally for some golden anniversary or other. Gudrun was so charming—enchanting, really. And Ernst-Ulrich has such a way with comedy. It was mesmerizing to watch. A bit later, Gudrun serenaded us with Schumann's *Papillons,* and near the end of the evening she accompanied Hildegard and her step-daughter in a lovely ballad about Rita and Karl, written and illustrated by their father. Veritable mountains of tarts and rolls, not to mention some excellent champagne, made for a triumphant evening on all accounts. Aside from us, there were a great many other relatives in attendance as well: all of the aunts and cousins from Hildegard's mother's side (the Rüdels) and Rita's father's side (the Steigerers, from Mainz), as well as from Aunt Lissy's mother's family (the Schikels, the Bonsels, the Brandenbergs, and the Selbachs). Of course Elsbeth and Richard were there too. They seemed to have a good time swapping jokes with a tenant in Rita's house, Herr von Bodebeck, who is a most entertaining fellow. Once little Gerhard and Fee had gotten wind of the fun, they joined in as well, followed by Gerhard Sr., who delivered a couple of particularly nice jokes from his repertoire. And Richard gave a delightful speech his light, humorous, and yet warmhearted

This is where the page ends. How did it get into this book, and how did this book get here? Mysteries both, but this time the right sort of mysteries: not worthy of pursuit. I don't want to know who wrote this letter or to whom it is addressed. Although I know none of the people mentioned in it—come to think of it, the name Selbach does ring a bell; his first name is Eckhard—there is something about the glimpse this text offers: it's as if it's real, happening right now. It sticks, burrows into me, and begins to spread, as new vistas open before me. Its perspective shifts to the guests' daily life, for which the party is a culmination, and then into their pasts, their futures, their children's futures. Now I am getting cold. I go back to my bed and lie down. There is still an empty bottle in my hand, and I set it on the night table next to me.

I wanted to learn more about Tynset, but I find myself asking why. What did I actually want to know? What, of the very small amount of information actually worth knowing, do I not know already? Or rather: I don't want to know what is worth knowing. What can really be communicated from a description of a thing or a place? Nothing. There is no sight, no view out of the kitchen window into the backyard, where bed sheets wave about gently on the line in front of the chicken coop with its crudely nailed frame and wire stalls, a rusty tricycle missing the top half of its bell, an abandoned watering can, and behind the coop a thick, but desolate forest; no snow on the ground or in the air, not yet; still no snow to cover the dust and the watering can and the tricycle and all the forgotten things of summer, to cover forgetting itself, and to enchant what lies beneath—none of this is in the guide.

What should I expect from Tynset? Not a single bird has ever been sighted here—but at the same time there have never been any battles. No Battle of Tynset. And as far as I know, no singers of Wagner have ever been born here either. There is nothing to document or depict. Sounds can be depicted, but silence cannot. Storms? Yes. But a light draft of air that brushes the grass between the stones? No. A revolution? Yes. No revolution? No. What happens? Yes. What doesn't happen? No.

Off to Tynset, then?

A long train ride on which I can't quite see myself. On the final stretch, perhaps,

transferring in Hamar, the sweeping curves of the branch line, and then a bumpy ride upward through the valley. Short layover in Elverum, this I can see. Waiting at the open track for the train in the opposite direction, yes—but it's the first part,

the first part, no. I don't see myself any more on the main tracks of the giant rail network, nor do I see myself in the bowels of a microscopic worm as it creeps up the crust of a medium-sized sphere, which is itself moving at blinding speed—

—in the fading light of evening, I can't seem to find myself in the smoking or the non-smoking section, in a growing layer of sticky grime or dust, leaning on a shred of tooth-colored lace that separates my head from the leather seat. I see myself neither alone nor across from the other passengers, all with their fixed goals: daughter's marriage in Bad Kissingen, association conference in Bad Rendsburg or Lausanne—and it is neither too hot nor too cold, and outside it's dark. There is nothing in the window save for a dim reflection of the train car's interior, everything once again: the space and its occupants, the spendthrift, the military judge, currently off duty, fat philanderers on the hunt, and grandmothers who don't look the part, no, and behind them pictures of the Mädelegabel and the Naumburg Cathedral—

or in the sleeper cabin, tucked under the night as we press on toward our common destination, the wool blanket pulled so tight across the mattress that I have to keep my feet pointing both to the right or both to the left, or one to the right and one to the left, but never straight up as one would lie in a coffin, pressed closely together so that the big toes touch—no, this I cannot see,

I cannot see myself being carried over the tracks, or hear myself rattling in the grooves, rushing across the bridges, and echoing into the evergreen forests—

I cannot feel myself being carried into the big cities, the capitals, sliding into the anatomy of the metropolis, the train station its intestines, perpetually filling and emptying. I cannot hear myself clattering over the crevices formed by intersecting lines, where the tracks split or cross, the bumpy field, the battlefield, peppered with flickering lights, but it is not me who skirts its edge, along a black wall, a muddy street, with scabby, rusted façades in the distance, with dead holes and lights glaring upon the eternal damnation that resides there, selecting new victims with each passing generation, an ever-growing number meeting their end. Past all of this and into the echoes of the halls, stifled screams, frozen sobs, and a crust of grime growing upward, mixing with the water and dripping downward again, onto the platform and onto the trains in which I cannot seem to find myself—

Regardless, I want to go to Tynset. My desire is hardening, I cannot escape it—

despite the fact that, in the end, Tynset won't be anything more than a confirmation of what I have always suspected, and what I have known for a long time: that I exist in a world of monstrosities, seemingly free, but in reality a captive. It is a captivity filled with hidden acts of abuse that often—no: sometimes resemble acts of affection, but for which we must pay dearly. In a cage, devoid of possibility.

Or were there possibilities? No, there were only illusions of possibility; I was in a large room that was in constant flux, shifting with the reflections of illusory possibilities, which in reality were nothing more than deceptions. All deceptions, yes, deceptions, the sea, the wind in which I stood, alone—or the wind in which we stood together—the billowing blond hair—or other moments—the labyrinth, for example, in the great big park in the mountains—no, they weren't mountains, they were hills, the Euganean Hills, yes, that's what they are called: the Euganean Hills. The park belonged to the Villa Valsanzibio. No, the town was called Valsanzibio. But what was the villa called? Am I now beginning to forget the background of my own life? And the landscapes? That would be the end.

It was Villa Barbarigo. No, I haven't forgotten such things, not yet. Villa Barbarigo. But the villa wasn't there anymore—it had disappeared, time had devoured it. Here and there you could still find uneaten scraps, remnants of stables, faded and crumbling—but the park, with its long, rustling alleys, and the labyrinth, the park was still there, straight-lined and impeccably kept, just like it probably is today. To think that all of this still exists—

there it stood: the labyrinth, in a long, late spring, its narrow, deceitful alleyways, wide enough for one person only, were lined by walls of yew, tall as a man, in a fresh, dark green, sharp and straight, as vertical as a plumb line, the corners trimmed to an edge so keen it could cut—no wind, just a cushion of fresh, cool air hovering above. A handful of young people, most likely students from Padua, were running down the paths, but they couldn't find each other, nor could they find the way out. Laughing, they screamed instructions back and forth: a sinistra, a destra, diritto, sempre diritto, dov'è, sono qui. They were laughing, yes, but it was a dry-mouthed laugh, as if their eyes were not laughing along, as if they had been laughed out. After a while dusk set in, the park grew darker, and the foliage blacker.

The students continued their fruitless quest, running wildly in search of one another. They were not laughing anymore, but they kept on screaming back and forth as the exit continued to evade them. Finally the night watchman arrived, accompanied by his dog. He climbed up onto the balcony overlooking the labyrinth and studied the scene with the seriousness of a general surveying his troops in battle. After he had gotten a clear picture of the situation, he barked a couple of orders to the students below, who were now standing in silence. He threw the riddle's answer down to them, and slowly they began to emerge, one after the other, sober now, their eyes clouded from the brief moment of terror they had just experienced, as if they had stared death in the face. It is very likely that they had done just that.

And as for me?

I was in the park as well, on an avenue lined by cypress trees. I heard the laughter and screaming from afar, and I was on the balcony looking down at the tops of their heads, and I was in the labyrinth, in all of the passages at once, wandering about, inside and outside, over, under, I was alone and I was with her—

—with her? But who was she? She had a dark voice, she said, "komm, es wird dunkel," or: "come, it's getting dark." Or was it "fa buio"? No, that wasn't it; I don't remember a *u*. It was an *a*, dark—dark—. What color were her eyes? I don't remember anymore, I've forgotten, just as I have forgotten her name. The only thing I can still recall is the background, the scenery; the actors have since vanished, changed clothes, transformed. Maybe they assembled before me and took a bow, smiling courteously. But if so, it was a moment I missed—maybe my eyes were closed. I should have been applauding.

No more of that, no more pictures, no conversations, and no voices. None of these moments—they are in the past now, forever past. Here is where I am lying, here are my beds, here is my house where I am staying. Should I ever leave this house, it would be to go to Tynset. I will leave it for no other reason.

Tynset, my only plan, the only possible goal. Otherwise I am without a plan, and without a goal, I am without guilt—or perhaps it would be better, safer, to say: without significant guilt—and therefore without responsibility. I don't have anything to make good again, nothing to wipe clean, at least not that I know of. As far as I am aware, nobody has suffered on my account. I carry no burden, save for the burden of life; I have no vision, save for the objects I see within these four walls, and the walls themselves; I have no sound, save for the sound of my heart and the crowing of the rooster; I am alone, without company, save for the company of my furniture, my wonderful winter bed, surrounded by faithful four-legged companions: two armchairs, hollowed out by years of sitting, and my night table, my good friend, ageless, always at my service, always carrying what I require, silently handing me the objects that occupy my nights, and then taking them back again. I don't often look to see what lies inside of my night table—perhaps I am afraid of what I might find, somewhere deep, evidence of an unresolved issue, or an accusation stashed away from long ago, which continues to live on despite its old age. Instead I prefer to reach blindly, rummaging around for nail clippers, pipe tampers, objects I sometimes possess in great numbers, and other times not at all, glasses, cans, tubes, and bottles, remedies for sore throats and raw skin and headaches, remedies against the by-products of life, its ebb and flow—all relatively tolerable, not harmful until they become so, with or without side effects, before or after eating, to be chewed dry or to be swallowed whole, with a small amount of liquid or a lot. And interspersed among them are the cuff links, valuable pieces of an inheritance, that have not been used for a long time, passed down to the end of their line, an illustrious past behind them and an uncertain future ahead. Where will these pieces go from here? Who will be my heir? The wine bottles are empty, as are the packages of tobacco. There is dried residue in the bottom of the teacup and a brown border on the

rim. The ashtray is full, as are the refuse areas, by which I mean
any horizontal surface, covered with objects set aside and laid
down, yesterday and years ago, newspapers, magazines, and on
top of them the telephone book, one of many, heavy, flexible,
easily toppled—when it falls everything else falls with it.

My night table, my faithful nocturnal friend, I stroke it,
touch it—

and then the telephone book begins to fall, taking with it the
timetable and a heap of newspapers. An accumulated load of
yellowing events comes crashing to the floor—paper evidence of
dwindling interest in these days, in these so-called events—and
waits in a pile for me to take notice.

Just as well; this will give me a chance to do some refurbishing.
I pick up a newspaper from on top of the pile, unfold it, and see

a picture: a landscape with two figures: the Minister of War,
or whatever he was called in the vocabulary of yesteryear. It
was a term coined to skim the foam from a seething unrest,
and to let it cool—the Minister of Defense kissing the hand of
the Cardinal. The Cardinal has since been called back to his
god, the Minister not yet—a close-up shot taken from afar. The
scene takes place at an airfield. In the background an airplane,
probably ready to start at a moment's notice, even if this is not
recognizable from the photo, ready to transport one of the two,
or perhaps both, church and state, through the air toward a
common, earthly, destination. At any rate, this appears to be
a pre-arranged meeting of sorts, for it is not very likely that
Cardinal and Minister would happen upon each other at a place
like this, a hub of mass transit, purely by coincidence. Maybe
their paths were pre-arranged to cross, a plan worked out in the
last possible minutes, and its realization documented.

In his left hand, the Minister is holding his black hat and a
pair of sunglasses, which he removed while walking. With his
right, he grasps the Cardinal's hand and, with his arm slightly
bent, lifts it to a height that allows him, with a slight tilt of the

head (making his already short neck even shorter) but without much of a bow (his sense of reverence would have allowed for more were it not for the limitations of his considerable girth) to bring the ring within close proximity of his mouth. But in reality he simply pulls the hand horizontally, bringing it a few centimeters closer so that the Cardinal's fingertips almost touch his chin, which places the ring not under his lips, but more in the vicinity of his lowered—seemingly closed—eyes. They aren't actually closed, though, but narrowed to slits and focused intently on the ring below them, as if they are trying to assess its worth, which they likely are. They are assessing its symbolic value, behind which the material worth—which is by no means small—is hiding. And the lips, while pursed, are not actually poised for a kiss, but instead for a smile, lending the Minister's face a decidedly impish quality that belies the feigned humility of his silhouette. As it continues to spread above the ring, the smile reflects nothing but pleasure, pleasure at the opportunity to perform such a pious deed in such a public place, in front of so many pairs of eyes, even if only to receive a cursory blessing, which the smile's owner doesn't need. For the threads that bind his fate are of a far different origin, tied securely to the earth below him. At the same time, the Cardinal's blessing is not something he wishes to go without. It adds spice to his dish, making it much more savory for those who must partake of it. A clear case, no secrets here.

Likewise, the Cardinal is barely aware of the blessing he is allegedly bestowing upon the shiny bald head and corpulent body below him, at least not at the moment. He willingly relinquishes his hand, but it is almost as if he wishes to pass the Minister a stack of files, while ignoring the kiss entirely. Instead, he seems to have directed his gaze over the bowing figure in front of him and into distance—not into the beyond, though. His eyes are focused on a very specific point, a point where something is happening, luring his attention away from the Minister and his pursed lips. But he is smiling—he is always smiling when not in prayer, mostly in forgiveness, but sometimes in pain as well, because there is so much to forgive. He smiles at the point in the distance as if he has made a place for himself over there and is looking forward to occupying it soon; not a place in the aircraft standing by, but one that is entirely unreachable by such conventional means of transport. This is a place just for him and his own kind: a fixed point on the horizon—and the line running from his nostrils to the corners of his mouth, and the smile with the automatic mechanical latch, measured with meticulous care and set with precision to the degree most fitting for the situation, betrays his fixed determination to defend this place at all costs.

Then it occurs to me: perhaps it is not a place at all, but a revelation, an insight that appeared before him precisely at this rather inopportune moment, right in the middle of a public encounter, hovering before his eyes with astonishing clarity, a doctrine he had pondered long and hard, but that stands before him now in its perfected form, the form in which he will present it to his infallible lord and master. Perhaps this is the reason he is in such a hurry, why the Minister seems to be an inconvenience—and now I remember that it was he, along with a couple of Spanish colleagues, who advocated for a new dogma, a dogma that would come thundering down to Earth as if from nowhere and refute Galileo once and for all. But it is still in the works, deep within the conclaves they are still filing and tweaking, refining. The sun really *does* revolve around the Earth—

and now, the Spanish contingent will not rest, the brothers from Seville and Valladolid and Burgos and Salamanca, their corpulent bodies protruding from under sashes of changeable taffeta. They have glimpsed the opening and are determined to squeeze one more through, to see Philip the Second ascend into the heavens, which would be well received by their significantly thinner, pince-nez-wearing German brothers—under the condition, of course, that they would be allowed to send one of their own as well, one of their crusading adventurers, to accompany the Spaniard in his ascent. They have also succeeded in garnering the support of their American colleagues, but only in exchange for one of the men who exterminated non-believers and scattered his seeds of faith upon the empty ground, a Cortez, or perhaps a Pizarro—enough, enough!

What else is here aside from my winter bed, my wonderful, valuable possession, in which the great murderer lay, the great insomniac, lonely, cruel, misunderstood, incomprehensible, by no means a procrastinator, not a Hamlet, but a doer, a wrong-doer?—in which he lay and watched, a bass lute in the grasp of his long, Gothic fingers, strumming and listening, his gaze fixed in the distance, where he found nothing, his gaze remained empty.

Aside from my bed and my four-legged companions, there is also my kneeler. Like almost everything else in this house, it likely belonged to my uncle originally. Where he got it, I do not know. I can only say that he was not a praying man. I don't pray either, but I decided to pull it out anyway from its place among the sewing machines, harmonium, dollhouse, and other junk littering the storage room, clean it, polish it, and set it up in my room. I believe Celestina uses it periodically while clean-ing, when the need to pray befalls her. I, on the other hand, content myself with observing it from my bed—not because it's particularly pretty, although it is by no means ugly either. The beauty is not what captures my attention. Instead, I prefer to pay attention to the person who is kneeling and praying—I see the fatty, meaty backside of the king of Denmark, I am Hamlet, I see my uncle Claudius, cowering before the kneeler or slipping from his perch, rolling on the floor and praying in an effort to free himself from his crime. But I do not kill him; I restrain

myself, I do not act—others act, but I do not. I peer over their
shoulders at his back, I listen to his breathless, whispered, sputtering prayer, the words tumbling from his mouth and shattering
on the floor, or hovering in a plume, mindless drivel, stinking,
smoking, smoldering, like Cain's prayer—

—no. Not that, not Cain's prayer. Cain's prayer didn't smoke,
and it didn't smolder. It was a good prayer, a proper one, for it
did not ask for anything. Perhaps one of the last good prayers—I
could be wrong about this—but certainly the first. But alas, it
was all for naught. The god to whom the prayer was directed
had other things on his mind and chose to ignore it. This doesn't
reflect poorly on Cain per se, but instead on his god. And why
did God not listen? This is a question that has occupied me for
quite some time. Even now, I cannot seem to read past it, or let
it escape from my ears. As if from nowhere, it appears in red
between the lines of a book or a newspaper. It was the first true
riddle I ever encountered; it made me stumble and fall. After
a while, I stood up again, bewildered and hurt. I had not been
expecting a riddle, at least not here, so near the beginning, so
early. I kept going, a little slower than before, limping slightly,
but trying my best to disguise it, ashamed. I turned around and
there it was, grinning and staring back at me—obviously I was
not the first to have fallen in its trap. This was something the
riddle did often, and something it enjoyed doing. It is still grinning today, sneering at me from under all of the other sneering
riddles. But it was the first, the original. It was also the original
injustice, the source of God's guilt, the God who, for no reason
at all, withheld his grace from Cain and scorned the fruits of
his field—letting them smolder into swaths of smoking soot,
making their grower cough so hard he could barely breathe—
while honoring the steaming flesh and blood brought to him by
Abel. Slaughtered in the name of the Lord, every part of these
animals—innards, intestines, and all—was lifted up on high,
and their shepherd showered in blessings and praise. For Abel
knew his god well; so well, in fact, that he was able to read his

wishes from his face: God wanted meat. It's as simple as that. For Cain, these fickle moods and insulting displays of favoritism were almost unbearable. He had always taken his creator seriously, loved him, idolized him. But now it was too much, and in his darkest, most frightful hour of disappointment he lashed out at his brother, God's pet, and killed him. Yes, this is how it went, and from then on, Cain was condemned to suffer eternal damnation.

It is written that Cain had a rather fiery and jealous disposition. Abel, on the other hand, was mild and pious. But who actually wrote that? The jealous farmer and the virtuous hunter and slaughterer: Cain, an evil and begrudging man, Abel, a good and just soul—no, that's just not good enough, I simply don't buy this configuration, not from their creator, and certainly not from the chroniclers—I don't know if anyone would buy it save, perhaps, for those question-hating consumer unions. I ask, and my question echoes through the house, through the night—I imagine that even Celestina must have heard it. I ask: what, during Cain's time, were the objects of malevolence, envy, malice, deceit, sinister desires, and impure thoughts? The Earth freshly created, populated by only four people, two already punished unjustly, their lives forfeited; what sorts of objects, what sorts of thoughts could give rise to this brand of evil? Where were the walls on which its tendrils grew, and the holes in which it nested? Where was the limb it started to devour first, before spreading out and consuming the rest? Nowhere. There was nothing but an illusory paradise and a desert and the blatant injustices of God's vendetta against Cain. A heavy burden, a blemish, a mark on the forehead, one that sticks, but not on Cain—no: on his creator. Enough!

Enough of this hand, enough of the game! What did I want again? What was I after earlier? That's right, I wanted to go to Tynset. But not by train. By car, and soon—as soon as all of the roads are drivable.

I should listen to the road conditions report. Road conditions report—not a bad term, if you think about it. Expresses itself clearly, and even has a certain metric rhythm. Road conditions report and snow report and avalanche bulletin—that's the best: avalanche bulletin. It sounds like a whole lineup of catastrophes. And why not? Do not all avalanches have their own names and pre-determined appearance times? The Great Marianna, for example, the valley's foremost avalanche—she can be expected in the late winter or early spring, around the time of the first snow melt. But there are also a few that arrive in the early winter, also with names, leaving mounds of snow strewn across the roads. Occurrences such as these are not dangerous if you're expecting them, and they generally have a way of announcing themselves, a light wind, perhaps . . .

I will go to Tynset, then. It's settled—well, almost settled. It's already late November, so I really should depart soon, before winter sets in, and before I lose the nerve to go somewhere—well, *that* nerve is already long gone. Tynset is the only possible destination. I will do my best to avoid all other cities on the way: Prada, Chur and Stuttgart, Hannover and—

Was it Hannover? Or was it Dortmund? Düsseldorf? Maybe it was Braunschweig. I am losing the ability to differentiate—maybe it was called Friedrichsruh or Groß-Gerau. I remember it was some sort of state capital, but I have no idea for what state. All I know is that I didn't want to enter this city; I wanted to pass it and continue on my journey, north or south. I was driving on a small, provincial road with cracks, potholes, tears, lacerations, scabs, and no shoulders whatsoever, but it wasn't any of this that bothered me. Not that I had opted for this route, no—I generally prefer the mid-grade roadways, a grayish-brown compromise between the frenzied turmoil of the highway and the creeping isolation of country paths, luring travelers from point A into the unknown—at their own risk, of course, painfully aware of each jarring bump.

And it was on just such a road that I found myself, with no

expectations whatsoever, master of my destiny and my vehicle. Nearing a small settlement, which seemed to draw its life force from an uncompromising desire to be as ugly as possible, I came upon a detour sign directing me off to the right. I obeyed, and as I turned, the quality of the road immediately deteriorated. I continued on, following the yellow arrow through intersection after intersection, sometimes turning to the left, and sometimes to the right, powerless at the spiteful hands of authority, which no doubt took considerable pleasure in reminding me of my subservience through the strategic placements of these flimsy signs. The detour was clearly marked, but I had long since lost my sense of direction—I had no idea how to get to Hannover or Braunschweig or Friedrichstadt, not to mention how to get past these places, which was, after all, my ultimate goal. And as the sun started to set, I realized I was now traveling in exactly the opposite direction from the one in which I needed to be going. This did not sit well with me, not at all. At the time, I had been prepared, within reasonable limits, to concede to the whims of the anonymous authorities, but not, like some others, to the degree of all-out submission. So, at the next turn, I took my leave of the detour signs, turning left where they said to turn right. As I veered off, I could feel myself slipping from the pull of the current, and my freedom returning. But somehow I had also managed to steer myself onto an even shoddier road than before.

I still was not headed in the right direction, but I was relatively certain from the predictable straightness of the road that I would eventually come upon an intersection, giving me a choice of two more directions, one of which would be the one I needed. And indeed, it was not long at all before just such a crossing presented itself: a little ways ahead was a street running perpendicular to the one I was currently following. I turned. The condition of the road itself was similarly decrepit, but, as I was able to make out from a mileage sign, at least I was now heading toward whatever inescapable place it was that I needed to pass through in order to continue on my way; Düsseldorf or Dortmund—I'll just call it Wilhelmstadt for now, because regardless of which capital city I was actually approaching, this name fits. After reading the sign, however, I couldn't help but notice that I didn't feel any more reassured. If anything, my sense of unease had grown stronger—from this point onward I could no longer give in to the fallacy that I had so easily managed to overcome the fate to which all drivers of this region (even the defiant ones) fall victim. To make matters worse, the road I now found myself on was little more than a dirt track: wheel grooves cemented in the dry mud, with patches of hemlock sprouting between them. All around me, nature seemed to be lying in wait, biding its time for the perfect opportunity to recapture what was lost.

After a few kilometers another sign appeared on the right: "Wilhelmstadt, State Capital," only there was no city to be seen. Instead, both sides of the street were lined with what can best be described as urban attempts, unmistakable signs of beginning: warehouses, torn-down posters, chain-link fences, wires, trash, dented canisters, rusted buckets, bicycle tires. Behind them were various demarcations for garden plots, and even farther back stood a cluster of industrial buildings: a northern German wool combing company, Veith Rubber Works, Boehrich & Schiesske Printers, Föttle & Geiser Gas Ovens, Dörpinghaus Chemistry Labs—all of these places form the backdrop of my childhood, and all of them I can remember by name, while the foreground seems to be vanishing before my very eyes; where these buildings had once stood there was now nothing more than a gaping expanse of fields; weeds grew unchecked between the beaten wheel tracks. Reacting to a projected need for expansion, the state capital had likely seized this land so that no other city could make use of it.

In the meantime, the street had gotten better, sturdier—there was even asphalt now. Gas stations started cropping up with greater and greater frequency, and in the distance I could see the future beckoning me forward. A street sign for the Ernst-August-Ring, the planning of which was necessitated by the surrounding terrain, and then another for Julius-Möller-Straße, which I could already make out in the distance, followed closely by Hermann-Riedel-Straße. This is where the city really began. Every German city has a Hermann-Riedel-Straße, and it is always unmistakable: rows of identical houses on each side, built by the enemies of architecture—utterly devoid of color, and without even the slightest attempt at refinement, these structures are shamelessly ugly. What's more, they are pervaded by an aura of security, an assurance that nothing will disrupt their current state of existence, barring the unforeseen mercy of a natural disaster. But until that day comes, they will continue to stand in unabashed plainness, undergarments hanging from recessed balconies, bicycles and tricycles leaning against doorways, and cars parked halfway on the sidewalk. The corners are rounded off slightly by restaurants and pharmacies, points of intersection with crossing streets, Schumannstraße, Friedrich-Zelter-Straße, Marschnerstraße—the musicians are arrested at the borders and called out by name. Muthesius-Straße marks the beginning of other areas of specialization, which extend along Otto-Herter-Straße all the way to August-Bötter-Straße, where I was now driving. Soon thereafter I came upon the very first stoplight, blank, but ready to light up at a moment's notice and direct the sudden bursts of traffic.

Now I was truly in Wilhelmstadt. I saw another sign with "Wilhelmstadt" on it, but this time without the additional "State Capital" designation. I drove into the stream of traffic like a twig being sucked along by a strong current. Cars were coming at me from both sides, and then from the front as well—I was flanked, I was an obstacle, the target of irritated glances and threatening advances, but I kept driving anyhow. Chlodwigstraße—a relapse, a barren strip leading to the switch yard, the entire area had been scraped raw by municipal waterworks and brick gas plants, by access and service roads, and to top it all off, a slaughterhouse. But eventually the roughness faded away, coming to a halt in front of a green belt. Chlodwigstraße managed to jump over this small hurdle and, upon reaching the other side, was promptly ennobled to Bismarckstraße, which grew into Kaiserstraße and emptied into the financial district, before vaulting upward to Theater Square, which, aside from the National Theater, boasts a fine museum of home décor. I continued on, trapped between swarms of taxis and cruiser ships, whose drivers guided them with unerring sureness and purpose. These people seemed to know exactly where they were going, exactly where they belonged, and they steered right for it. And there I was among them, the lone traveler who knew neither where he was going nor where he belonged, searching only for the distant, my path determined by signs or arrows or traffic workers waving me along, devoid of will, ignorant of my goal—I drove past Bonifatius Square, down Breite Straße, past the warehouses and monuments, Stephan Square, Rudolf Square, staring straight ahead to keep myself from losing my way and to avoid making eye contact with the driver beside me at the next red light. True, sometimes they are gazing off into the distance too, dreaming of being somewhere else, but oftentimes you find yourself alongside a thug, or a murderer—I have glimpsed many a horrid past while waiting at traffic lights. I continued straight ahead, but my path was diverted by a policeman waving me in a different direction. I tried to win my route back as quickly as possible, but to no avail—Breite Straße narrowed into Bürgerstraße, which turned out to be a one-way street heading in the opposite direction. I made a right-hand turn—I had been hoping to turn left, but the one-way sign forced me to go to the right, chasing me and my freedom onto narrower and narrower alleyways until I finally reached the core. I was now in the Old City, in the crook of the Dyke Ditch, at the Burghof—no, on the Lower Ried, on the Lärchenberg, where the old city ramparts stood, preserved for over five centuries to trap the likes of me. I was on the Upper Schießschanze, squeezing myself into the Judengasse, where I belong. I watched as I got stuck on Ziegelhüttenweg where it turns into Kleine Düwelgasse, although it was not until Am

Rothen Speltz that I was forced to turn back. I put the car into reverse and drove back onto Rumpligen Spieß, where I made a left turn onto Sonnigen Speltz. From here I was able to continue downhill, passing Am Althentheil, Pognergasse, and Kothnerstraße. As I drove, conditions improved, the street grew wider again, and a traffic light glimmered in the distance. As I got closer to the intersection, I saw Friedrichstraße extending in both directions—I could finally breathe again. I turned onto Hamburger Allee and was greeted by the scent of acacias as the vast expanse opened its welcoming arms. As I accelerated, I quietly slipped past a delivery truck driving slowly and regally in the right lane. On its side was a company name: Wehrgenus & Flatow, Delikatessen—it was like a message. Soon, everything became quiet. Villas shot by on either side, their sprawling gardens stretched into blurs before me—it was much less populated now. The road started to sink, and suddenly I came upon another sign: "Wilhelmstadt, State Capital." And there I was again, at Herzog Adolph Square, Stephan Square, on Breite Straße, Theater Square—the Home Furnishings Museum was now on the other side. I turned right, but could not manage to avoid Bismarkstraße—or a view of the National Theater's backside, for that matter. Ifflandring, Schillerstraße—Ifflandring turned into Schillerstraße, that is—and then Scharnhorststraße, Gneisenaustraße, but it was all the same to me. I continued driving and felt no fear upon seeing the Home Furnishings Museum for a third time. I was able to recognize the building by the various objects surrounding it but was hardly relieved upon realizing that, although they were the same objects, this was a different establishment, a different street, and a different square—I had made progress. There was that delivery truck again, Wehrgenus & Flatow, only this time it was headed toward me from the opposite direction. I continued onto Husarenstraße, and then Sedanstraße, which was closed off to all traffic going straight. I turned left onto Marschnerstraße, hoping not to run into Nikolai or Brahms, but they didn't appear. Instead there was Zilcherstraße, which eventually broadened into Pappelallee. I started to see street signs with the name of a place beyond this state capital, a place that had been on my original route, a faded star of my former hope. But on another sign, pointed in the very same direction, was the name of the town I had just left. I drove until I reached a detour sign, which, along with the two towns I just mentioned, listed many others, in all twelve cardinal directions. Temporarily absolved from the responsibility of choice, I followed the arrows, crossing the west and east beltways. The buildings assumed a rougher, unfinished quality as suburbia sprung up around me in the form of restaurants, pharmacies, and furniture stores. The city was slowly relinquishing its hold. I drove slower now; I could feel myself relaxing. On the right there was a sign for "Wilhelmstadt, State Capital."

But I didn't turn around—even if this were the capital, it was undeniable that I had just come from there. And so, for the third time, I crossed into Wilhelmstadt. At first it looked different—I hadn't come upon Grävenich Square before—but after turning onto Hamburger Allee, which I was now following in the opposite direction from before, things started to look the same, and I prepared myself to retrace my path once again, to spend the rest of my life on these tangled streets, to breathe my last breath behind the wheel. I turned onto a narrow street called Abtsgasse, but that didn't seem right. I kept going, awaiting the inevitable appearance of the Financial District, the Lower Ried, the slaughterhouses, the Home Furnishings Museum, murderers, and the service roads. Briefly taking my eyes off the road, I caught a glimpse of the Untere Schiessschanze bouncing by my window. But the suburb I was now entering, despite being identical in appearance to the one I had crossed through earlier, had different names. The restaurants were now on Gustav-Freytag-Straße, while the gas stations ran along Theodor-Körner-Straße—I was among the poets now. The colors changed to a grayish-white as Perlmoser Cement Works rushed by, a pulping company from Lower Saxony, Diegenhardt & Pfählrich vacuum cleaners, Wohlbrück Installations—I had definitely not been here before—and then grass and dust. The street slipped down on the scale of upkeep; cracks appeared, and slowly turned to holes, buckles, sand. And before I knew it I was trapped in the clutches of yet another detour, ripping me from right to left—but also out. Finally I had escaped. Setting my route northward or southward, I just drove, leaving all of the capitals, Hannover, Braunschweig, Groß-Gerau, Düsseldorf, Dortmund, Altstetten, and Wilhelmsruh, behind. A burnt-out stoplight, and then no stoplights: farmland, country roads. I turned onto a winding gravel path—I don't know where it led. I don't even know where I was coming from, where I slept that night, or if I even slept— —

It must have been Hannover. Wehrgenus & Flatow, Delikatessen, that's in Hannover, 45–47 Bismarkstraße, faithful customers of my spice blends, especially #2 and #3.

Road conditions report. What was the number again? One-six-seven, I think . . .
a good pound of crumbled white bread, with the crust removed—wrong number, nighttime cooking, I've heard that gas and electricity are cheaper at night—*and then sixty to seventy grams of margarine or a similar cooking fat*—cooking fat, that doesn't sound good—*two level tablespoons of bread or potato flour, and then mix into a mass*—a mixed mass!—*over low heat, let cool slowly, and then shape into fist-size lumps*—no, that doesn't sound good—*drop into boiling water and let cook for five minutes, then cover with sour cream or yogurt. Garnish with freshly cut*—
No, not that—that should be different: copper skillets, iron pans, and on top of them a glazed, crusty dome, peppered with cloves and sage. A splash of Gewürztraminer so that it hisses—or perhaps a Chateaubriand with the black checkmarks of a steel grill, a dollop of green-speckled herb butter on top, like a tennis ball hitting a racket—these are the things that endure.

There are minutes, quarter-hours even, when aromas such as these can instill a sense of comfort, make one forget feelings of displacement; in moments like these, life becomes a station on the train ride of time, a tangible piece of present between the hungering past and the satiated future; the tongue licks, and the teeth bore into a juicy morsel of reality, thoughts sit heavily in the mouth, lingering in the space between the gums and the lips, but cannot be swallowed. Instead they rise up again and settle once more in the skull, soberly looking down upon the meal as a past occurrence, from which nothing remains but a dead animal, antlers without an owner, an empty space in the stall.

Road conditions, avalanche bulletin, tangible, verifiable facts, more reliable than forecasts, unalterable, a cycle: roads, passes, yesterday, the first snowfall, drivable with enough momentum, snow chains rattling like the treads of a caterpillar, pressing slowly but steadily onward. The person to follow me will make it through as well, as will the next, but the third will get stuck— like Mr. Wesley B. Prosniczer that one time—the tires will not catch, and their feverish spinning will turn the snow to ice. Yellow fog lights—what a beautiful image that evokes: fog lights—Tynset—groping for the snow ahead, piercing it. And so I continue up and over the pass—

but not down again, farther, I push off from the road and hover above the snow. The ground is growing smaller and smaller below me as I set my course for the Milky Way—or in the other direction, south, down into the narrow valley, where the river washed away half of the street last summer—or was it the summer before that?—down among the pebbles of the river bed, I pass over the crumbled, splintered roads, open wounds, with patches of hard scabbing scattered across the surface, down into the valley of floods, and then farther still, farther south, slipping through the weather to some faraway beach where not a soul is to be seen, only water and sand and the unending furl of a lazy wave, driving a trembling mass of foam toward the shore that collapses onto the beach like a soufflé. A jellyfish, perhaps a sea nettle, is left in its wake, but before long it too dissolves, leaving only a smell behind to accompany the tangle of seaweed and half of a cigarette pack, now full of sand. I can feel a slight breeze.

No, none of that right now. Not now. Besides, I'm getting tired. It's nearing twelve o'clock, which means that soon I will be one day older. Then I will sleep—

—the red wine bottle does not fill itself—but I wish it would—

—sleep, when I can. I am not a good sleeper, I never was, and now I am even less so. It used to be that I didn't miss getting sleep. In fact, I used to find it just as inconvenient as I now find the waking hours—I am awake far too much, but it's not the sounds that keep me up, it's something else—what is it?

It's a matter of outsmarting sleep, of positioning myself just so, so that when its vapors waft by they are lured by the tiny fleck of skin I have exposed for their capture. I'm trying to absorb something of sleep's essence, something that will spread out inside of me. Most of the time it's only a thin layer, which does not last long; I awake soon thereafter and must then find a new method, a new morsel, spiced in a new way to whet sleep's appetite and keep it satisfied—provided, of course, that it deigns to grant me a visit at all. Each method can only be used once per night, after which it must be returned to the card file in exchange for another. But there are also times when, upon reaching for a new method, I come up empty-handed—my options are growing fewer and fewer. There are many that I have only used once, and that have since disappeared into thin air, lost forever. And then there are others that I have used multiple times—memories, for example. But memories are hypocritical. On the surface they appear welcoming, but it is only after one lets them in that they shed their veil of warmth to reveal a harsh and disturbing core, whose malicious sneer never fails to drive sleep away for good.

This cardinal—I remember now that I saw him once: on the morning in question, I just so happened to be in Rosenheim, and the cardinal was there as well, although his visit was likely less coincidental than mine. At any rate, this chance encounter allowed me to witness a few moments in his daily routine. He was walking at the head of a long procession of black-cloaked followers, shrouded in a mist of untouchability. As he strolled along—no: his steps were invisible, almost as if he were float-ing—as he bobbed and billowed down the street, spewing incense from all sides, he ran his hand through a young boy's hair, whispered a blessing to an infant in his mother's arms, and bestowed countless other tokens of grace upon the devoted followers lining his route. Holding his hand vertically, with his thumb pointed toward his chest, the cardinal allowed his head to sink into the perfect incline of humility, as if expecting a ray of light to burst from the heavens at any moment, but know-ing at the same time that he was a sinner among sinners and was not worthy of grace. Perhaps the reverent slant of his head would allow God's blessing to slide down his body and onto the ground, into Rosenheim, where it would touch all but him. He also spoke here and there, to mothers and old men, with a tone of unending sympathy, which was meant just as much for himself as the person to whom he was speaking. These people were his companions on the journey through mortality, and as he spoke to them, his words seemed to say: soon you and I will have overcome this existence, and in God all things will be better. But until then, we must persist, and we must carry what has been laid upon our backs. He then directed his gaze forward, a look of painful transfiguration on his face, and concentrated on the horizon, where a tiny black dot was just visible, exactly as he had done at the airfield—only this time the point was actually a vehicle, a heavy black limousine driven by a man in a cassock. He walked up to the limo and got in so he could ride off into the distance, casting blessings from the window as he went. A heavenly gust of wind kicked up a cloud of dust behind the departing vehicle and then dissipated in the midday air. Suddenly, it was just Wednesday again, and the cardinal was gone. If I remember correctly, he had come to Rosenheim for some sort of christening.

Twelve o'clock. The hour of aging is past.

Eyes closed, the back of my head sunk deep into the pillow, palms down, thumbs pointed inward, my arms rest alongside my body, on top of the covers. This is how I travel through time, and how I lie in space,

lie in this bed, in which, before me, nobody had lain for one hundred twenty thousand nights. I bought it from some rich boy who had inherited it from his parents, and was in the process of auctioning and selling as many pieces of furniture as he could to clear the attic for his model train set. According to what he told me, the set consisted of some eighty thousand pieces—but he would easily make it to one hundred thousand after a little while (his hair was gray, by the way), or even one hundred twenty thousand. Eighty thousand parts of a model train set, whose owner had descended from an ancient line of Neapolitan royalty. To think how his predecessors had heaved, grunted, and driven splinters into their hands, all to get that bed out of the basement and into the attic in order to make room for the wine, which had to be moved there because the Spaniards had seized their lands, their vineyards, formerly owned by the cousins of kings, the brothers of cardinals, and even the nephew of a saint, by princes whose ancestors had moved this bed, with its faded gold ornaments and crumbling wood carvings and cracked trim out of the palace's State Chambers and into the basement because there was no longer any room for it, because they wanted to replace it with softer, lighter beds that would be more pleasing to the guests, beds with canopies and lascivious Cupids and sculpted posts and salacious symbols and silken curtains. This way, they thought, their indiscretions would be more charming and refined, more gallant than the sinister acts of their predecessors—for the brightly lit evenings and darkened *levees* of the new generation, the bed of a murderer, and a double murder, was just not suitable. It was a heavy piece of furniture, with a frame made from solid walnut. The canopy was wooden as well, and on the inside, in a place visible only when lying down, there was a small painted skull, put there by the first owner on his fifty-third birthday, which was also the year of his death. He had painted it there to remind himself that he was a murderer, and that he would not stop being one until the day he too ceased to live. On sleepless nights, he would look up at the skull and be filled with memories of the horrible deeds that took place in that very bed, in the bed of death, the bed of love, the bed of indiscretion, the bed of unfaithfulness, of deception and adultery, the murder bed, the bed of remorse—

he lay here, in this same bed, on a night like this one, a November night, here, where my head is right now, right here, tilted slightly to the right—no, not tilted: fallen, battered, a head, the head of Princess Gesualdo, Maria Gesualdo, attached to the carcass by the spinal cord alone; the stiletto that was used to slit her throat is still buried somewhere east of Naples, rusting under a layer of earth. Here, where my body is lying now, this is where her body was as well, covered by a nightshirt made of lace, soaked in her own blood and the blood of the man lying sideways on top of her, his lifeless head resting against her forearm, here, where my forearm is lying right now, his stomach pressed against hers, his arched back pierced by a halberd. Here, where my legs are, this is where his legs were as well, the legs of the Prince of Andria, bent at the knee between her splayed thighs; here they lay, the couple that had been so beautiful in life—*sorprendente bellezza*—perhaps even as beautiful as Paolo and Francesca—freed from their final embrace, his genitals slipping from hers in death's curt interruption; the way their limbs were entwined, it looked as if they had been in the middle of a dance, although now the scene was rather a tangled mess: bone knocking against bone, disheveled, matted hair, four smeared hands, twenty fingers frozen in a final, horrific spasm, four eyes opened wide, as if the final moment of terror was still to come, two gaping mouths, four lips crusted with blood—the echo of the excruciating, two-voiced scream of death had long since faded, trapped and suffocated by a bloody gurgling, and now nothing but silence in the darkness,

and sitting silently in the darkness, next to this bed, my bed, are the voiceless witnesses, untouched, uninvolved: an extinguished candle on the floor, above it a chair upholstered in a dull satin, and on top of the chair a steely glove, laid aside only to be picked up again at any moment; draped across the chair back is a woman's doublet, ready to be put on again at any moment; a little farther away, a curtain ripples noiselessly near the open door leading into the anteroom. The anteroom is empty, and the flickering of the fire has died out. The door into the next room is wide open, as are all of the other doors marking the path of the echoing escape, through the palace wing and into the open air, the park, the courtyard, and the streets,

and in the rooms not even a sound, everything is still, the screams of the fleeing chambermaids have faded, the steps of the murderers died out, the clattering hooves in the courtyard have dissipated, the torches have been extinguished, blown out on command, in a single breath, all in anticipation of the horrors of morning—

only the murderers do not wait, they are already outside of the city, riding furiously upon two gray horses, whose nostrils are steaming in the cold air—Gesualdo, who has left his own palace wide open behind him, casts the stiletto with the blood of his wife over his back. His accomplice, whose halberd pierced the prince's back, is named Pietro Bardotti, by now they are far away, and the morning is drawing nearer, bringing with it a sheet of cool, bright air that streams through the gaping doors and causes the curtains to billow gently and something in the courtyard to start rattling. With it comes a damp and translucent gray, casting soft shadows into the rooms and illuminating the various colored objects: I can see now that the chair's satin upholstery is the same shade of dark red as the dried blood on the dead bodies; the doublet is yellow, and the glove is silver; from the horrific scene before my eyes, a still life begins to take shape, a still life made of dead bodies, of dried blood that knows not to whom it belongs, of pieces of furniture that are now heirlooms, a still life still undiscovered, cold, frozen behind the façade and the dark shadows of the palace windows that look down upon the streets of Naples, the city of the site of the act that was carried out on this very bed, the bed in which I am lying right now, and in which I may soon fall asleep.

Tynset. It lies in my mind like a seed strewn between lines of thought, nestled on a patch of flat land between rolling hills and a desolate forest, and then pressed into the ground. After a short while it sprouts roots and begins to grow, sprawling like a weed, climbing like a vine, and suffocating all other thoughts except those about itself. It spreads wider now, occupying other regions, and grows taller, attaches, becomes independent and demands charter, which I deny: I have not come to that point quite yet, and will not for a long while still. Yesterday perhaps, before my hour of aging, but today, not yet . . .

It lies between Hamar and Støren, or more accurately and more beautifully: between Elverum and Røros, where a steaming, wobbling passenger train traveling from the southeast to the northwest passes through with a clattering echo, but without so much as a glimpse of its twin heading in the opposite direction; before they get a chance to meet the two are separated by a signal-studded passing loop positioned at the halfway point, in an expanse of open fields, the faster brother gazing into the distance, waiting, but never seeing, separated without so much as a greeting.

A station where silence reigns except for during a storm, when the tin warehouse groans, or the gentle crescendo that begins five minutes before the arrival of a new train, the measured movement during its layover, and then the quickly dissipating decrescendo of its departure—otherwise there is only the occasional resounding thud from the two freight trains standing idly on the holding tracks, or a casual exchange of words, accompanied by the jingle of small coins at the buffet, which, thanks to the Scandinavian alcohol restrictions, is a truly dull affair.

What else? A couple handfuls of houses—all, or at least most, made from wood—in which it is still quiet; the inhabitants of Tynset have cut themselves off from the same cold moon under which I am lying at this very moment—assuming, of course, that it is a moonlit night. If not, then it is just as dark there as it is here, save for the couple of streetlights illuminating the lines on the road, vanishing lines, whose faraway endpoints are invisible in the darkness. Tynset can never be completely dark, for while the blackness of night may serve to obscure the trivial and the superficial, it allows more mysterious qualities to shine forth, qualities that Tynset still possesses—

even if only for me. For others it's just Tynset, and for most not even that. And none of the people sleeping behind the wooden walls—not the couple gyrating ecstatically in an effort to conceive a child, not the farmer who feels the first chills of death in his bones, nor his two sons, who stay up late into the night dividing his plots amongst themselves, and not the teacher, who, tortured by his woefully underdeveloped, undereducated hometown, makes calculations to assess the feasibility of building an adult education center—none of these people know who I am, or what Tynset is to me. No wonder. Even I don't know it. A point of anchor in a sea of delusions.

The people of Tynset don't ask questions about Tynset,

neither the sleepers nor the wakeful, neither the dying nor the heirs, nor the teacher. Well, perhaps. Perhaps the teacher does. I'll try with him—I should attempt to establish some sort of relationship with an inhabitant of Tynset, at least one. If I take the teacher as my friend, what will he think? He is a free thinker, this teacher, a member of a poorly paid, frequently abused caste. He thinks:

No. Nobody is expecting an answer. Everything is already an answer. Nobody asks because nobody knows that you even can ask. They all grew up with the answers, the teacher thinks, but not with the answers to questions—no: these are false answers, answers that enable one to get ahead of the questions, to impede them; these answers are designed to smother the will to ask before it even blossoms, to cover questions as if they didn't even exist. In the beginning there was the answer, my friend thinks, and only then the question; it says so in the Bible, in the eleventh book of Moses and in the Gospel of Luke and the Gospel of Frederick and the Epistles to the Corinthians, volume 5—and when the question came, it came as the poet did to the great distribution of worldly wealth: too late. There was no longer any room for the question, the teacher thinks to himself. Grinning, spruced and starched, in choir robes and cassocks and stole, in tiaras and miters, with crooks and rings, and stiff neckbands and black puttees, eyes gazing tranquilly, veiled behind rimless spectacles, their voices soft, their gestures round, and their songs glorious, the men of God sat upon the boxes in which the answers had already been packed away, ready to be shipped off into the world. Grinning, they pointed to the addresses. The packages were devoid of any markings that might indicate the fragility of their contents, for the men of God knew they could trust their carriers.

These are the thoughts of the teacher in Tynset, my friend. Or are they? Yes, they are.

Tynset. It doesn't make sense to try to sleep right now. I'll get up, I'll get up and go find another bottle of red wine—this means immersing my feet in the icy mist that hovers above the ground and setting forth once more through the house. But this time I will get farther than the library. No tomfoolery this time, no operetta guide, no droning idiot, no charlatan, no Jung, no interpreter or seer or Jesuit priest, no wise man or keeper of the keys, no chronologist or publicist shall stop me this time, nobody, nothing will stop me from wandering free through my own house among my inherited and acquired possessions, feeling, floating, like the sleepwalker that I am.

Yes, I am a sleepwalker in the truest sense of the word. The only difference is that I do not sleep while walking—I am a waking sleepwalker, clairaudient as one can only be in the pitch of night. I wander through the house, knocking on the glass plates of the barometer, behind which things are always changing; I peer into closets and boxes and bookcases at silent portraits or silver-tongued relics; I find a lock of hair in the dust—but whose is it?—in an old vase is the key to a clock—but which clock? when did it stop?—I inspect the landscape on the wall and am suddenly transfixed; I stand and listen to the sound of the invisible crickets, waiting for their wings to fall; or I stand before the framed blackness of Jean Gaspard Muller and guess; I follow the gaze of a young, unknown Florentine, but whatever it was she saw is no longer there, maybe it was never there,

I go into other rooms as well, but I don't turn on any lights—I want to continue my guessing game. I grope for objects in the dark and am groped by others, like the nightly wanderer von Erlenzweig—in an attempt to learn fright, I retreat, but this is something I have already tried to learn and simply forgotten again. I feel a lance point graze my skin, but I continue on, a hand reaches for me in the dark, but I do not allow myself to be caught, I pass by, skimming surfaces, rough or soft or stiff— —

Where was it that I saw a drum from Zanzibar with dark human skin drawn across it?

and where was it that I saw human-skin lampshades, made in Germany by a German craftsman who currently lives on his pension in Schleswig-Holstein?

I continue through other rooms, take a lachrymatory from the shelf, even though I am not actually crying, not anymore; I turn it around so that a new set of etchings is facing me; I stroke heads: the head of a stuffed curlew, two identical shrunken heads from the Congo, where they kill twins; there are some things I don't even see, even though they are looking at me, while I see other things for the first time—it seems I am always discovering the unknown, and that the unknown is discovering me.

After all, I was not born in this house. Instead, I am expanding from within it, taking its possessions for myself, while it takes mine from me—and if I die in this house, only then will I have been born in it, if death will be so kind as to erase my other memories. But I don't think he will be that kind—death is seldom kind because he seldom has to be.

It's been eleven years since I moved in, although it was actually several years earlier that I got the idea to do so. But let me be more exact in my thinking: I intended to move into this house ever since I inherited it. Ever since I've been here, however, I feel as if I am *still* here, increasingly cut off, the circle in which I live my life growing constantly smaller, and my actions within the circle more limited—most days I don't even touch the shrinking boundaries.

The house has remained the same; I've added very little and changed very little. What I really did was take it over, and along with it came Celestina. But Celestina has changed, and she continues to change right before my eyes, consuming herself, wasting away, drinking to the point of drowning.

I've inherited nearly everything—save for the few objects I acquired myself on account of their inherent mystery—inherited it all from an uncle, or somebody I called uncle; to be honest, I'm not exactly sure what his official title would be; first cousin once removed, perhaps, or twice removed: I believe he was my mother's cousin or maybe her mother's cousin, unattached, unmarried, without any ties to emotion or duty. His was a planned loneliness, and everything was working out splendidly. He didn't have a job either, and as far as I can remember he didn't particularly want one. He kept himself busy by recording what the world had to tell him through its physical matter, its processes, and the phenomenon of life by measuring what there was to measure and notating what there was to notate, and similarly by recognizing what could not be measured and what could not be notated, but without ever drawing any sort of conclusions— not from the measurable and not from the unmeasurable, and not even from the fact that the measurable is measurable and the unmeasurable is unmeasurable. The house was, and still is, full of clocks, calendars, barometers, each keeping track of the other, of hydrometers and hygrometers and thermometers, a measuring instrument in every room, even in the stairwell, the basement, the storage room, and the shed—an abundance of readable displays to help him perceive the perceptible and arrive at a prognosis of its effects; arrows, pointers, mercury, scales in millibars, Celsius, Fahrenheit, Reaumur—it was my uncle's mission to be able, at any time, to dispel even the slightest trace of doubt regarding air pressure, humidity, date, day of the week, hour, temperature, as well as current and future weather conditions; in all of these matters he strove for a sense of absolute clarity, even when various readings and interpretations were possible—in my uncle's life, considerations such as these

served as a vital precondition of an orderly day. Three times a
day, morning, noon, and night, consistent to the minute, he
scurried, later ran, then walked, then limped and hobbled, and
finally dragged himself through all of the house's rooms and
hallways, carrying a giant list in which he recorded all of his
measurements in vertical columns; he then assembled the lists
and organized them by year, bound them, and eventually hauled
the volumes in piles to the shed. But he never stopped recording,
measuring, and documenting; even when he could no longer
move from his bed, when he could feel death in his body, he kept
up his practice, maintained his lists. As death bore down on him
even harder, he enlisted the help of Celestina, who would read
the measurements aloud from the makeshift lists she compiled,
allowing him to make the necessary additions to the official
documents. Near the end his markings started to make less and
less sense, they became undecipherable riddles, and then he died
during a night when the temperature read nineteen degrees
Celsius; in the library it was sixteen and up high in the loft
next to his telescope it was only eight. He didn't live to note the
temperature in the morning; on his deathbed the thermometer read fourteen degrees, with an air pressure value of seven
hundred sixty millibars—these final measurements had been
recorded in Celestina's handwriting. Her acts of reverence had
outlived the revered, who was actually nothing more than a
heretic in Celestina's eyes, a man risen from the depths of hell,
who, despite his Catholic upbringing, had contemptuously
rejected the performance of his last rites: "Don't touch me!"
he had screamed as the priest approached. Despite all of this,
however, Celestina's loyalty for my uncle endured all the way to
his grave—she did not stop her list-keeping until the earth had
settled around the body, bringing the life of her lord to a soft,
fading end and sparing him the violent shock of a single blow.
I said "her lord," although what I really meant is "her master."
"Her Lord" means something different. "Her Lord" does not
walk through the house, but is omnipresent within it, in every

nook and every cranny. "Her Lord" does not read barometers but instead creates the conditions they register—that is, if you wish it to be so. And despite everything, Celestina wishes it indeed.

I knew this uncle not only when he limped and hobbled but when he still scurried as well, when he was spry; I saw him scamper from room to room, through doors, cracks, and holes, behind curtains and tapestries—he was a shadow, silent and weightless, a finger pressed against his lips, an urgent hand stretched out to silence any potential sound or utterance, to arrest any movement, to force nascent words back down into the throats of their speakers. This is how he moved through the house, forward, sideways, springing, crouching, listening, watching, a magnifying glass in his pocket and a tripod under his arm; under the other arm was a Bunsen burner, and a stopwatch and a compass hung from a chain that he wore around his neck. He was always on the hunt, always hot on the trail of something unexplained, always forging ahead into unknown territory, quickly, before whatever it was he was after escaped him and disappeared. And it always did disappear—that was part of the plan. Futility was the apotheosis to which all of his efforts built, the only part of his routine that never changed, for he knew that he simply didn't have it in him to expand the boundaries of research and knowledge. But this was not something he even wanted to do anyway—he was perfectly content with feeling his way forward only to get stuck somewhere along the path, for this somewhere was his home base, his refuge. It offered him a good vantage point from which to gaze contentedly, with humility and devotion, at the road he had traveled—upon which the shroud of mystery was descending once again—as well as the grandeur of the unknown terrain still ahead. He rejoiced at the sight of both, for it pleased him that so much of the world was measurable, and that there existed so many reliable instruments to measure the measurable, and that there was no need to put any of it to use; he ran through the house like a child, barely able to contain his excitement about what he would see next; he presided with sovereignty and justice over his instruments, never once expecting the impossible; he sat in a state of sublime abnegation, denying even the tiniest urge to analyze—a fast runner, a just ruler, a patient sitter, a great abnegator, a contented admirer of all things, measurable or not.

Most of the paths eventually lead into the storage room in the back, the part of the house where the stone fades to wood, the great, dusty room full of galleries, stairs, ladders, and skylights, full of junk and forgotten objects—it is easy for things to get lost here, and
    in the beginning I got lost here myself, here, where my house turns from three stories to one without the roof getting any lower. But now I know my way around.

And during my nightly wanderings I very often find myself being led back there. It is a long, angular route: from my winter bed I must pass through a total of six doors to get to the north-west entranceway, where I must then slip past the gaze of the murdered king of Denmark before finally crossing the threshold into the cavernous wooden hall, a realm that stops its breathing to embrace me, a dry, stifling room devoid of movement, so still that even the most timid of creatures would not want to remain in it alone, church-high, but not churchlike, more like a caravanserai: one over the other, three wooden galleries extend around the perimeter, while the dark canopied walkways that connect them—which are supported by staircases, beams, and banisters—provide caesura-like interruptions. Standing in the middle of the room, it feels as if you have stepped inside of a tall tower, whose roof is so high that it almost vanishes from sight. The entire place is full of discarded objects, the lighter ones rising ever higher while the heavier pieces remain on the bottom; a harmonium, formerly owned by the pious wife of a slave trader, built by a company named Greetgebouw, Jericho,

New Jersey; the bed in which my uncle died; a child's playpen, still assembled, the only evidence of a childhood spent in this house—but whose childhood?—a chest with iron buckles, full of engravings and albums; and everywhere the floor creaks under the weight of feet, stairs, walkways, galleries, banisters; there is even creaking in the loft; and cement begins to crumble, wedges start to loosen, and nails start to slip; everything is becoming undone, and yet nothing collapses; the entire house is suspended in a state of perpetual undoing, waiting for a signal, perhaps my death, to fall to the ground at last and bury my memories in rubble—at least here they would be well preserved.

I wander into this room on many a nightly journey and climb up to the telescope, past the admonishing reminders of repairs long overdue, past the broken glass, the crumbling plaster, the wooden planks bundled together for a long-forgotten project, the bottle jackets and bottles from long-expired vintages, early late-harvests, the splotchy birdcages, the sacks of birdfeed—which will feed the mice into eternity—the mouse traps, and, as if to taunt them, the fresh mouse droppings, the piles of rusted nails, organized according to size, hammered straight again by a compulsive saver, a chance insight into another side of my uncle's character (which is reconfirmed by the bundles of string and wire), the long temperature lists, faded ink on yellowed paper, the weather lists, divided into two columns, predictions on the left and actual conditions on the right—this was my uncle's way of hinting, in an entirely friendly manner, without the slightest hint of malice, at the incompetence of professional meteorologists and the limitations of the scientific method; bundles of letters, remnants of lives gone missing in the foliage of a dead family tree (or one that is dying in me), cards, stamps, the material grows smaller as I get closer to the loft, thinner, lighter, swept up by the wind of time and carried in a billowing mass to the rafters—

but at the very top, covered in dust on the very last stair, there is another solid object, a small, but bulky, heavy, flexible book bound in black, a hymnal, placed there by me, and not once moved, the last reminder of my farewell celebration.

Farewell celebration, a curious party, and the last one I ever gave. It was not originally conceived of as such, but was instead meant as a technical etude of sorts—no, not that either: more of a test, an attempt at recommencement after a period of inactivity; to be clear, this is in no way suggestive of a resolution to persist after having recommenced, but at the same time, there were no plans to stop either. The party didn't reveal itself as a farewell celebration until everything was over—the absence of arriving headlights in the dark winter night, the air cleansed of its former bustle and clatter, the rooms emptied of guests and filled with the traces and prints of their uninhibited actions—until I opened the windows and released the drunken mist into the night air. After that night I never saw any of the guests again, none of them, save for the evangelist, whom I stumbled upon the following spring, halfway up the pass, contorted and frozen inside of his dead vehicle, in the snow.

It was a harsh winter, and no sooner had the invitations been sent out than it became relentless, threatening to block all of the roads leading to my house; the pass was not drivable, and the only other access road, a sweeping detour, had been covered in so much snow that it was at times indistinguishable from the banks on either side, a loosely knit web of snowdrifts in the fog where cranes landed to rest when the visibility became too poor to fly. But the guests came anyway—perhaps the difficulties of travel had served to sweeten the prospect of arrival, perhaps they were attracted by the thought of meeting each other in an unfamiliar setting. Some of them had brought others along as well, and some of the others still others. But this did not concern me—the formation of the guest list had been somewhat of an arbitrary undertaking anyway, if not downright inadvertent.

Even then, the names were already starting to disappear from my mind, bearing only a distant association to their owners; and then the owners started to disappear as well, their features blurring, bleeding over onto the features of others—I mistook three people for one, and one for two. Today there remains nothing of the faces, figures, or names. Now I think that perhaps the party was an attempt to counteract a sense of reluctance, reluctance concerning my deficient mastery of the great card game, the one that everybody else knows how to play so well:

sitting around the round table, they study their cards with a calm concentration, passing, playing trump cards, defeating and being defeated, and then I come and ask: "Who shuffled the cards?"—they look at each other in silence, taken aback by my simplemindedness. Finally one of them answers: "The cards, my dear, have already been shuffled by the time they reach the table," whereupon they all laugh and I walk away—I won't be joining their game, I can't even play it. I don't belong here.

Sometime after midnight a young woman—I remember that her profession had something to do with matters of taste, and that she was correspondingly good-looking—expressed a desire to see my telescope. Whether or not this is actually what she wanted, I do not know, but, out of far-sightedness and rationality, I took her at her word. I had already abandoned any intention of putting a stop to such an adventure—were it to present itself—or even of catching hold of its tail as it ran off; I could already see the skull emerging from behind the flesh, and the urge to undo what had been done grew ever stronger inside me, while any hope of stilling it began to fade. To me, the desire to have a look at the stars didn't seem at all out of the ordinary, which meant, of course, that I assumed others would feel the same. I allowed the young woman to hold my hand and lead me from room to room, all the while taking great pains to remain the follower and—here lay something of a weakness, which I may have hinted at already—to appear as such. Out of the library and into the gallery, past the couples and the groups of guests and into the hallway, from which Hamlet's father was absent—he had been scared off by the guests and had indignantly retreated to a more secluded spot—and then up the stairs to the corridor, door, anteroom, and finally the door to the storage room, which opened with a creak. The young woman already knew where the telescope was set up—all of the guests knew before they had even entered the house. Upon arriving that evening, each of them had glanced upward in search of the opening in the roof—I can still hear their exclamations of amazement upon spotting it, as if this tiny irregularity in the house's architecture were some sort of bold and unusual statement.

We stepped into the wooden hall and I turned on the light, a single bulb for the entirety of this cavernous, labyrinthine space. It hung uncovered from a horizontal support beam, its cable in violation of every conceivable safety consideration, and managed to illuminate only the right corner of the room, while making the galleries on the opposite wall appear even darker, like catwalks in a murder play. Quiet and stillness washed over us, a stage full of props, from which the players had vanished—

the door opened behind us, we had been followed, and as we began climbing the first of the staircases, even more guests trickled in, buzzing in anticipation of unexpected sights, continued festivities—Belshazzar's Feast, perhaps, with fiery script singeing the walls—or maybe just lascivious observation. We struck up a polonaise, an exodus, pairs, groups, funneling through the door and swarming into the hall, their astonished eyes immediately drawn upward in an attempt to gauge the height of the roof, yelling and screaming to test the wood's acoustic properties, before fanning out into vertical and horizontal configurations that slowly infiltrated the room's many niches and spilled onto the galleries. There was an excitement reminiscent of journeying to a faraway island, only here nobody seemed intent on discovering anything new—the night's entertainment continued in the manner it had begun, but now in an altered setting. On the whole, the change in scenery proved to be a welcome development, with the sharp decline in seating quality having a rejuvenating effect on the partygoers—the group's volume remained at a hushed murmur as their voices groped about in the darkness, feeling for the walls and the banisters,

from which they would never return. There was no echo here— the door to the storage room had been closed, which meant that, all of a sudden, there were new factors at play. A sense of unease began to spread through the air, grabbing at the guests as it passed by, and one by one they spoke a little louder, laughed a little more dryly, as the room's less charming elements became more apparent; as the journey descended farther and farther into cobwebs and splinters, many started to wonder what we were even doing here in the first place;

they sat miserably in the darkness (or in some cases in the dim glow of the room's sole light source), in the sound-deadening dust, the flimsy walls and dust-covered drapes muffling all attempts at communication—

they sat and stared at each other, drink glasses migrating from person to person like a ring dance around a hollow core, in which I stood with my companion, but high above, like rulers of the underworld, Persephone leading Hades ever upward toward the stars—I stopped and looked down upon my realm, upon the murmuring, undulating mass that now filled the formerly silent hall; it was defenseless against them, and they passed through its innards with fluid-like ease—

in actuality, the hall seemed dead to me, lifeless despite the life teeming inside of it, a hollow corpse, crawling with hungry parasites eager to feed on the bits of flesh still clinging to its skeleton—the room came alive, but its inhabitants were dead, ghosts, a horde of lemurs; I felt a stifling claustrophobia rise through my body and squeeze my lungs, robbing me of breath—I was a Hades who wished his kingdom to be empty; I was afraid of the room, of its fullness, afraid that this party would go on and on into eternity—

—all of a sudden I feel an urge to return to the storage room, to taste its silence, to be reassured of its emptiness, shining my light in its corners and recesses like a night watchman; I think I'll go—
    and take the empty bottle with me—a bit of red wine would do some good I think. I have been thirsty for quite a while now and have put it off long enough. My body is in need of relief.

Tynset—doesn't that sound like Hamlet? Yes, it does sound like Hamlet—how strange that it only occurs to me now. Like Hamlet, yes, that's it, "there it lies"—"ay, there's the rub!"— There it is, indeed—ay—ay—

I stand up and put on my slippers, for the how-many-th time? This time I slip into my tattered robe as well, for it is cold. With my flashlight and empty bottle in tow, I embark once again on my nightly rounds, beginning with the library. I don't bother to turn on a light—I won't be in here long.
    —through the library and out onto the cold stone of the hallway, and there he stands, stiff and silent, Hamlet's father. I expected nothing less. There he stands, waiting for me, but looking in the opposite direction; he stands and waits for my little finger, waits to take my hand in his. But I pass by, ducking out of his view, I pay this apparition no mind, it has nothing to do with me, it's not my father, no,
    my father was different—

my father was a better man than this man here, and his ghost certainly does not spend time lurking around at the bottoms of staircases. He left this earth once and for all, without regrets. Unlike the man standing in my hallway, he doesn't have his eye out for revenge, despite the fact that his end was far more gruesome. No, there was no poison dribbled into my father's ear during the course of an afternoon nap. His was not a peaceful passage into the beyond but a violent demise at the hands of Christian patriarchs from Vienna or Weserland.

But this man just stands here, as if insulted. I find myself irritated that he is also named Hamlet. It was with immense hope that he had named his son, a hope that ultimately betrayed him—he deserved it—doubly betrayed him, in fact. Not only was his son nothing like him, but it was his son who became Hamlet, while he would spend the rest of eternity known only as Hamlet's father.

There he stands, a man's man, not a woman's. His stature is hard, straight-lined, and not at all erotic. He is the type who looks good atop a horse, but would not be the sort—I say this for the sake of fairness—to dismount with an elegant bend of the knee, or to strike at the leather of his knee-high boots with a riding crop. No, that would be a different breed of horseman from this one. He is, however, wearing riding boots, complete with spurs. His attire is sturdy and well constructed, making him in this regard not altogether unlike me. He is always bareheaded, but only for the purpose of demonstrating his faith—no matter what the danger or risk—to whomever may be looking down upon him. He actually is religious—"yes, I am a believer," he says, and then glances around as if to evaluate the effect of his confession. He pays no heed to earthly dangers and approaches everything with open eyes and a steady gaze. Yes, there is no other way to say it: with a steady gaze. When surrounded by friends, he scoffs at danger, and he has many friends. Enemies in his midst pose no threat to him. "Let them come," he says, or bellows—no: he says it, as he tends to say many things.

He does not wear any silk—partially because his father did not wear silk—but prefers leather and a vest with metal fittings, which he cleans and shines himself, for, as he always says, nobody can clean them like he can—the art of cleaning metal has become lost in recent times. When he was young things were a lot different, and for the most part better. He is bearded, hardened against wind and weather, loves to hunt (but is not "The Hunter"), and enjoys singing (but is not "The Singer")— mostly he sings ballades, of which he has three or four favorites, which just so happen to be his father's favorites as well. He is well loved, and guests at his table do not forget him for a long time—but after a couple of years they *do* eventually forget him, or rather: they confuse him with other similar rulers, but this speaks less against him, per se, and more in favor of the other rulers. —Even still: a man, take him for all in all—still—

still, one should not forget that he derives great pleasure from the jester Yorick, even if he can't quite follow him through to that last thought, that final reach for an exhausted metaphor. He is not a man for metaphors, but he doesn't hate them either—he understands their existence and is willing to accept those who use them, even those who enjoy them.

He is not a drinker but a man of moderation, although he does enjoy red wine—"my wine," as he says—in carefully regulated amounts. Regulated with equal care are the utterances he makes between sips regarding the various facets of kingly life. His speech never once cuts corners but instead marches carefully along the perimeter, methodically encircling the topic at hand. They are bland monologues, robbed of even the subtlest piquancy, and similarly devoid of illumination concerning the original thoughts in which they are rooted. True, roots so small are often difficult to illuminate. His speeches are received eagerly by those around him, but for me—what am I saying? Me?—I mean: for his son, Hamlet, the king's words seem distant and foreign; sometimes he wonders whether the topic might have had potential before his father commandeered it, but after bearing witness to such systematic treatment, he is forced to conclude that any former flame of possibility is now most certainly extinguished. At any rate, his father's topics of conversation feel foreign to Hamlet, very foreign. To be sure, he is a man with penetrating eyes—I said that, or something like it at least—but they do not penetrate any deeper than the shell (although this they do succeed in breaking), leaving the core untouched and unrecognized. The king doesn't even know that there is a core, despite the fact that he is holding the shell.

He is one of those men who only need four hours of sleep, but he is not one of those men who bore others with this information—he understands full well that the mention of such traits comes across as annoying to those who do not possess them. Never once, however, does he grant himself the luxury of sleeping past these four hours—he sternly denies anything he does not need. This alone puts him a world—the world—apart from his son, who, like me, is a passionate sleeper, but who, also like me, is just not built for the activity—like me, he puts off sleeping for long periods of time until he finally succeeds in finding temporary refuge in its shallow crevices; and like me, it is never long before he is sniffed out.

But his son is dead, and the unredeemed father stands at the top of the stairs, at the point in the house where the elements of the night become one, where it echoes and where the moon shines in—he stands there and looks down at me, waiting. I let him wait and continue on—unbolting the heavy door that creaks like the door to a tower—into the storage room, where the spices are drying. Perfumed air wafting over me, I climb the stairs to the highest point, and there it lies, the hymnal, gray with dust, in the same place it has been ever since the farewell party.

And here I stood, up here under the roof, among the rafters, stubbornly planting my feet while my companion persisted in her attempts to reach the telescope, peering down into the dark shaft below me, waves crashing against its sides. We were now well into the early morning hours, and the evening's zenith, whenever that had been, was long past—the alcohol-soaked dawn drew nearer, and with it came a beautifully uplifting sense of indifference to time and place, here and elsewhere, today or tomorrow, life or death. In this moment, all prospects seemed bearable, and the future just, perhaps even welcome—it was a moment that would cause anyone to embrace fate with happy blindness, to approve everything in advance, for there was nothing bad that could possibly happen: it was a state of reconciliation—I know it well—a state that ignites and extinguishes; drunkenness has the capacity to illuminate even the most foreign of guests—be they murderers or heroes—from the inside, rendering them as they truly are, in the flesh, under the skin, making visible the hidden trembling at the corners of the mouth, that ever-so-subtle weakness that the wariness of sobriety serves to obscure, or the flickering light of insanity behind the eyes, not to mention the myriad other telltale signs of the fight between reality and desire.

But this time I didn't see anything, didn't uncover any new secrets—looking down at the crowd below me I could only make out the tops of heads, which betrayed nothing of their owners' wishes or intentions.

Meanwhile, I felt the young woman's hand pulling impatiently at mine, and eventually I was forced to follow, high above the wooden landscape and the calmly undulating sea of human figures, poised to spring into action at a second's notice should one of them decide to try something new—it was not a state of expectation, per se, but rather one of extreme volatility.

Finally we found ourselves standing in front of the telescope; I put my eye against the eyepiece and started making the necessary adjustments,

when suddenly a cacophonous chord issued from the harmonium below, tinny, dusty, an even mix between the strident warble of a barrel organ and the breathless hooting of a rickety old church instrument, a whole note with a fermata, then a second chord of similar length, and then a third, at which point I was able to recognize the beginning of a hymn, wretchedly, pathetically out of tune, like the soundtrack to a silent film about the brutal trials of witches and heretics and their torture imme-diately thereafter—the F and the F♯ had gone dead, as had one of the low As; in their place were the felt-padded thumps of fruit-less keystrokes followed by a bony knocking sound. I stepped out to the gallery railing and looked down, as did several others, doubtlessly elected by their respective groups to determine who had come upon the horrible idea to test the old harmonium's keys like that—probably Richard or Max, who never seemed capable of leaving such things alone. At this point, so early in the morning hours, it seemed unavoidable that the incident would be followed by the performance of yet another, similarly inane act hailing from our less cultivated years, something that, back then, might have sparked a reaction, like Hans Georg's head-stand, or Henry's parodies of Rilke and Heidegger, or Marcel's drunken ritual of unveiling his crooked legs, the sight of which unfailingly brings him to tears, and which, as he always insists with truculent agitation, at this point fully consumed by the masochistic pleasure of public confession, are the real reason for his celibacy—despite how dull they had become, displays such as these were also expected, and were always, habitually, rewarded by success—

—but this time, no such performance ensued. It was an unfa-miliar figure at the keyboard. On top of the harmonium lay a panama hat, wide-brimmed protection for American summers, and next to it a black leather briefcase. The man was sitting on a chair that he'd pulled up to the instrument and playing hymns from which F, F♯, and A were noticeably absent—it was all so horribly out of tune, so dusty sounding, so bony, but a hymn is a hymn, and remains recognizable even in the worst of acoustic circumstances; in fact, it is sometimes imperfection that lends such melodies their simple but powerful fervor. From my vantage point I was not afforded a clear view of the mystery musician, who continued to play as if he had been hired, and I could see each of the other guests craning their necks in an effort to determine whether they had guessed correctly about who it was; the harmonium was positioned directly under where I was standing, meaning that I was only able to see the top of the man's head—for all I knew he could just as easily have been an invited guest as a friend tagging along. But then there was that briefcase, and the hat—before I knew it I was caught up in the same sense of wonderment that was sweeping through the rest of the crowd, gathering intensity as it traveled from person to person, climbing higher and higher until finally it reached the top, reached me—"What is this?" Soon, all of the guests were standing at the gallery banisters, and just like that the room was filled with a choir, peering down from above in anticipation of the organist's first note. The man stood up, looked around, looked up at the galleries full of people, laughed like a magician who had just pulled off a successful trick, bowed, and greeted his audience with a toothy smile: *"Hi, boys and girls!"* he shouted, and raised his left hand, palm facing inwards, to wave.

Not a single person answered; instead, they continued to stare down from above, a feeling of mistrust eating away at their former inebriation—their irritation was palpable, their faces expressionless. But the crowd's suspicion seemed only to encourage the performer, and to lighten his spirits even further. He raised his pointer finger, as if to say: "Just wait, I have something for you," opened the briefcase, removed a stack of black books bound in flexible leather, and set them on the harmonium. The pile quickly became the new point of focus for the bewildered onlookers, and remained such until the briefcase was empty. The man then stood up from his chair, picked up the stack, and began distributing the books through the crowd. He began on the ground level, carefully maneuvering between the mounds of junk and discarded building materials before climbing the stairs to the first gallery, where he continued to hand out the books, smiling the blindingly white smile of a benefactor serving a higher power, but not uttering so much as a single word. As he ascended to the second gallery, the anticipation grew, and the guests began to stretch out their hands—suspiciously but willingly, almost demandingly at times—to receive the leather volumes as their distributor made his way through the crowd; behind this act, they were sure of it, there must be some sort of hidden secret, a surprise, which, upon its imminent revelation, would likely be a disappointment. Gifts in hand, they continued to watch, as if the man's back would offer a clue—only when he mounted the staircase to the next gallery did they turn the attention to the book itself, speculating about the title, and, as they began to flip through the pages, conjecturing about its significance in this particular context, in this room, at this hour—with every new page came the renewed expectation that it would turn out to be something other than what it appeared to be. But no, the book was, and remained, a hymnal from the Evangelical Revival Movement. Followed by an expanding ball of silence encased in all manner of muted curses, the smiling man continued distributing his message of happiness and redemption, unperturbed by and impervious to the glances of the recipients, which he hardly seemed to notice. He smiled because he knew it would get worse, but then better as the users of the hymnal found themselves rewarded a thousand times over for their efforts. Finally, he reached the top level and made his way over to where I was standing—I could feel the angry glances of the guests converging on me, their host.

Only much later—just now actually—did I realize that the partygoers must have thought this act to be a planned part of the evening's festivities, my contribution, if you will—in fact, they may well have even come to the conclusion that the entire gathering had been some sort of elaborate conversion event: under

the guise of innocent fun, I had lured them into this room,
where a harmonium had been set up and to which a proselytizer had been summoned. And now he was standing in front
of me, holding out a black leather-bound hymnal. He stood
tall, and his presence was one of glistening weight, a mass of
securely rooted belief with closely cropped hair, a pale white
face, and ruddy cheeks, drawn tight by a youthful and joyous
asceticism, a non-smoker, a non-drinker; his small eyes sparkled
from behind a set of square, meticulously shined glasses with a
metal frame with a sharpness that had been honed during long
years of evangelistic work—there was a curious naïveté to him
as well, a smiling, but humorless mouth with teeth too white to
be real; a loosely woven nylon shirt, so white it almost looked
blue; a yellow necktie with a black cross stitched in the middle,
pinned to his shirt by a clip in the shape of crossed daggers, in
the middle of which the initials W. B. P. were engraved; golden
cuff links shaped like little crosses, with a blood-red ruby in the
center; a light blue Gabardine suit with gray stripes, casual cut,
providing copious room for notebooks and writing utensils; a
red carnation had been slipped into the buttonhole on his breast,
and his lapels were adorned with war decorations on the left and
various society badges on the right. He wore an enormous wrist-
watch, which displayed not only hours, minutes, and seconds
but the date and day of the week as well. His feet were clad in
soft, shiny, light brown half-shoes—everything about him was
summery, despite the winter, everything just so, just as it needed
to be in order to inspire trust and courage in what might otherwise be an uncertain faith; friendly, reliable, colorful, the only
thing missing were stripy socks, I thought to myself, black and
white perhaps. I stepped forward, bent down, and surreptitiously
lifted one of his pant legs to see if he was wearing them. He was.

He asked if me if I was the host, in thick American English.
"Yes, I am," I replied, also in English. He produced a card from
his pocket and handed it to me. It read:

Wesley B. Prosniczer
    Revivalist
        Chicago, IL

As we stood there, high among the rafters, there emerged a humming from below, cadences, shreds of words, fragments of uplifting phrases, the turning of pages, accompanied by sporadic attempts at two-part harmony—in all likelihood the decision to start singing had been arbitrary, and the intent of the singers, if there was one, predominately one of mockery; but no matter, Prosniczer reacted with a smile of satisfaction. His hands now empty of their devotional cargo, he descended the stairs with an agility that made me wonder whether steps were even necessary for him, hopping across the galleries packed with preluding guests like a well-practiced conductor hops up to the podium, fully aware of the effect of his lissome entrance. Now back at the bottom, he made his way to the harmonium, laid his hand on the top, and turned to face the galleries of onlookers above. He spoke loudly: *"And now, boys and girls, let' sing a little, shall we? I suggest we sing that wonderful wonderful song on page 49,"* whereupon the room was filled with whispered ruffling; even the young woman at my side turned her attention away from the stars—her mind focused on a different heaven now, she too began leafing through the hymnal in search of page 49. As Prosniczer struck the initial chord he was answered by the eager humming of a chorus testing its voices and searching for the opening pitch. After a short prelude, he raised his left hand and conducted the opening measures; the hymn had begun:

> One sweetly solemn thought
> That comes to me o'er and o'er:
> Nearer the great white throne,
> Nearer the crystal sea . . .

—and the entire room sang along, some off key and some with the wrong pronunciation; others did not seem to understand the wording, their mouthed syllables groping for a deeper meaning; some appeared hesitant, and others blushed, but as the music went on, their confidence seemed to grow; scanning the crowd, I could not find a single grimace—there were even a few smiles, but these were put on, worn for the purpose of demonstrating ironic distance and communicating to fellow singers that hymns, not unlike fine wine, require careful evaluation before a judgment can be rendered. There they stood, their eyes fixed on the book, or staring into the distance, or resting on Prosniczer, and there I stood, watching them sing, watching as something terrible made its way through the crowd: the unified action of a body of confessed sinners, overcome by the solemn desire to reflect—before my very eyes there arose a castle, a mighty fortress, its walls reinforced by heightened emotion and remorseful clarity; the night gave way to Sunday, and each member of the congregation looked himself in the eye, unashamed of the eyes around him. So delicate,

so delicate they all were, they all are, not only my guests, but everybody save for a few—save for me and a few others, but where are the others?—so receptive to the will of a man who can surprise and astound, who understands how to capitalize on the moment. It's true, the best parts of mankind are still bad enough—this realization hit me hard, rattled me, made me shiver, and still makes me shiver when I think back about that night.

True, it didn't last long. When the singing came to an end and Prosniczer stood up to begin his sermon, bringing his hands together, fingertips pointed outward, in front of his necktie, lifting his eyes toward the crowd above him, and saying: "*My friends—or rather let me say: my dear good friends* — — —"

when my guests were forced to listen and no longer allowed
to sing, forced to accept freedom instead of expressing it, to
be acted upon instead of acting themselves, the atmosphere of
uplifting redemption began to dissipate, and was replaced by a
cloud of displeasure—all of a sudden they felt betrayed, ashamed
of their premature willingness to be swept up in prayer; and as
the remnants of drunkenness wafted up toward my lofty vantage
point, inebriated contentedness was replaced by whispered anger
and rustling unease, amplifying by the second until Prosniczer's
words were drowned out, forcing him to unfold his hands into
gestures of placation. But this only turned anger into rage, and
it was not long before one of the hymnals came flying from the
disgruntled mob. It was followed closely by a substantially larger
volley as more and more of the guests were spurred into action
by the initiative of one.

Prosniczer's smile widened; now came the real test of his
commitment to faith. This initial, antagonistic backlash was
perfectly natural—so much so, in fact, that one could even say
it was part of the plan. He knew this reaction well from his
previous appearances at gatherings such as this, he expected it,
and even became skeptical in its absence—for such was the path
to true conversion: those who were the least willing at the outset
would one day become the most unshakeable evangelists, the
ones who would later be recruited as proselytizers. This had been
his reaction as well upon witnessing a conversion for the first
time. Thinking back, he even wondered why he hadn't thrown
anything at the man trying to convert him—

but when the guests started reaching for other objects,
planks of lumber broken into segments, nails, wooden wedges,
Prosniczer was forced to retreat behind the harmonium to save
his own skin, not to mention his belief. When he was no longer visible, the fury did not linger long on the instrument but
instead seemed to ricochet off of it, making its way upward, to
me. And rightfully so, I thought to myself—I still think this,
by the way—because by this point nearly everyone must have

thought that I had asked this man to come, that I too must be an active proselytizer for the Evangelists. Surely they now believed that the party had been nothing more than a deceitful pretense to lure them into one place, that the wine and the whiskey had been financed by the offices of the Revival Movement, a conversion banquet whose purpose had been, in one fell swoop, to lead an entire flock of new souls to their god, even if it meant a little drunkenness along the way—

the cursing grew louder, and the angry glares, shots of poison and spite from below, pierced my skin. Without uttering a word, the young woman pressed her hymnal into my hands— her desire to see the stars had faded and she began to descend the stairs. The beginning of the end. A glass shattered, a bottle tipped over, monosyllabic exclamations exchanged, and gazes averted: the hymn, the prayer, all of it had become a point of shame for which the only remedy was scorn. The hall began to empty like after a long-awaited concert gone awry. A muted hustle and bustle lingered for a while in the foyer as snow boots were tied, coats were buttoned, and complaints about the frightful weather were exchanged; and then it was out into the sobering cold: doors closed, footsteps dwindled, motors ignited, and snow chains rattled, but there was not even the slightest trace of a human voice, not even an echo; the silence of winter descended as if the party had never taken place, and the clock struck four, my rooster crowed. I was alone with the proselytizer.

He emerged from behind the harmonium, still smiling (he had probably never stopped) as the final hymnal connected with his right shoulder—it was my hymnal. Well, it was not really mine; it was actually the one the young woman had left behind. To this day, mine is still somewhere up there among the rafters, in the exact same place where I lay it down.

He played his part right up to the end. Yes, his dignity had been rattled, but he clung to it. Smiling up at me, he turned his other cheek and waited for the blow of the final hymnal. I resisted.

The fact that he had driven my guests away did not make me angry—I couldn't care less. In fact, I had already been thinking about how to get rid of them—it is not unheard of for such gatherings to persist for days on end, and multiple nights. To think of how many times I have carted a lingering drunk out of my house in a wheelbarrow and leaned him up against a tree along the road. Yes, in this regard Mr. Prosniczer had actually done me a favor. Despite that, however, I was still pleased at the accuracy of my first throw. It had been a symbolic blow against one of the world's great absurdities.

I also thought about Celestina, about her and others like her, standing there where they had been put, where they had been left, dauntless in their faith but daunted by its professional representatives, ruined by the clergy—but despite this, they would remain on the lookout for signs of redemption until the very end. And then comes somebody offering a cheaper alternative, coated in sweetening lies that make it taste better and go down easier—and what's more, it doesn't cost a thing. Celestina stumbles, falls, stands up, and drags herself forward before falling down again and staying down. Smiling and singing, the others float above her, transforming before her very eyes into fat little angels with palm leaves and golden teeth.

The last I saw of Prosniczer—of the living Prosniczer, anyway—was his smile, and the last I heard of him were his footsteps echoing through the hallways and doors, followed by the hum of an ignited motor and the spinning of chainless tires in the snow, the very same tires that would lead him to his end.

By the following morning, all of the hymnals had disappeared, save for the one that still lies among the rafters. Celestina had burned them. Right from the outset she had known what Prosniczer's visit was about, and that he had been all through the valley, from the pass all the way to the mouth of the river, distributing his hymnals—like hidden Easter eggs or hidden traps—at every possible location, from the local taverns to the hospital to the doctor's office to the train station to the post office. And at every location the reaction had been the same: the books had been thrown back at him. No, she said, he won't have any luck in this area. Everybody's already Catholic, and that isn't about to change. She said this with a beaming air of triumph, as if, for that moment at least, she were not a castaway, but a faithful inductee, relishing hour upon hour of heavenly grace.

And that was Wesley B. Prosniczer, a purely coincidental, yet absolutely indispensable figure in the game being played here. And when I think back on him now, it is with a distinct sense of gratitude, although I doubt that he understood the part he played in my life, the *diabolus ex machina*, if you will, the scarecrow that drove my guests from their all-too-comfortable perches atop the storage room galleries—this would not have been something he could comprehend. Even if he had borne witness to the ultimate effects of his actions, it would not have been an experience he could process.

And up here, high among the rafters, there lies a hymnal, as if laid to rest by a devout believer intent on returning. Up here, there is absolute silence—absolute, I tell you. Up here, I hear nothing, nothing above me and nothing below me, not a single movement, not even the thought of movement, with the exception of the occasional creak as the wood bends and cracks; some time ago, but not anymore, I also heard the sound of an owl in the night, the echo of its mournful call, a deep whistling—I don't know how they do that—I saw nothing, however, save for a pair of owl eyes, glowing like friendly warning lights illuminating the line that nobody is to cross. Some time ago, I'd say—sometimes—but not anymore, not for a long time now. This place has provided me with a haven from the dangerous currents below, a place to recover after pulling myself up out of the roaring throngs—there is less movement up here, less air, and every sound is muffled, but it is also calm, absolutely calm. The extra few meters of height make all of the difference. When I'm up here it feels like being in the emptied-out hull of an upside-down ship, a reverse ark. I am surrounded by ancient wooden scaffolding, its beams still jagged from the axe blows that created them—crude, but sturdy construction—and by bat droppings, and spider webs abandoned long ago by their eight-legged inhabitants in search of a fresh start; the decaying carcass of a moth—did it die suddenly, while fluttering around, or was it a slow expiration, a final twitch of the wing before that last bit of warmth was frozen away?—rusty tin cans, scattered across the floor of the loft like chess pieces, catching the drops of rain water falling through the cracks in the ship's hull,

and then onward, past all of this, I feel the pull of the current again, and air streaming in, sweeping through the rafters, which crisscross in the most arbitrary of fashions (by which I mean they meet where they meet)—up here there are different laws, the laws of the loft, unchanged since the Middle Ages, an unwritten code of honor, foundational rule of the Carpenters' Guild,

and then farther still, all the way to the last, outermost corner, the skylight with the rusted iron frame and broken glass, always open, for through it extends the arm of the telescope, which is supported by the dormer outside—no, not one of those new-fangled contraptions, but an old reflector model from back in the day, pointing outward and upward into the night, penetrating the stars.

It does not penetrate very deeply, but enough to make visible the rings of Saturn and the landscape of the moon. It is old—before me, it belonged to my uncle; he was the one who had it mounted here so he could gaze into the stars and between them, all the while drawing no conclusions.

Standing there in the corner it looks so cumbersome, its

TYNSET   111

features so helpless and outdated, its builder's pride rusting away. It is certainly not pretty—it hails from the age of cast iron, the age of cast-iron Chancellors, terminal stations, and benches on health-spa promenades, but unfortunately not from the age of engraved star signs, slender Roman numerals and symbols, and mythical world systems, the age in which instruments of knowledge were decorated while men of knowledge were banished or burned.

But it is capable of magnifying an object to sixty times its actual size, and magnification does not diminish over time. And once per night it becomes my destination—I can make it this far, to this, the highest, outermost corner of my house, but not a step farther, and I don't want to go any farther either, not on foot at least, but perhaps with my eyes and my thoughts. Upon reaching this point I stand still, my body grows roots, planting itself as if to remain here for the rest of eternity. Soon I no longer feel this body, not even the legs upon which it stands—there is no weight anymore, no rafters, nothing pulling me down, nothing binding me to this earth. Standing in front of the telescope, I am bodyless, gently turning the wheel and the crank and observing the changes with desperate eyes, adjusting the device that will bring this silent mystery into focus, bring it closer—there it is, before my very eyes, glowing and black and flickering and still and silent, signs that mean nothing, nothing more than a squandered answer, handfuls of facts sown into rich earth, from which nothing will ever sprout. Here I stand, burrowing ever deeper into the eternally unimaginable.

When the moon shines, I point the telescope at it and observe, studying it first from the outside and then getting closer and closer; softly, like an angel alighting for an annunciation, do I touch down upon its surface, standing on it, on this thing, this dreamed-up way station for adventurers with astronomical aspirations embarking on adventures of astronomical proportions, receptacle for worn-out jokes about moon-men—

I push off again, floating now above the surface, where I remain, perhaps at the Plinius crater, or gazing across the vast Mare Tranquillitatis—a shadowless expanse, a cold desert— behind it I can see Goclenius and Guttenberg, those cool and standoffish brothers, rising up in the distance; to the right, much nearer to me, I spot Arago, an afternoon's stroll at most, but one with neither rest nor allure, and certainly no nourishment along the way, no poppy-seed rolls; somewhere there is a place where childhood and childishness come to an end—this is that place, the border is here, and not a step earlier. And it is here that I stand, like a compass between west and north, shielding my eyes with my hand; I do not love this light, the harsh, permeable darkness of the sky above and the icy glow of the ground. I am blinded by the blackness of the shadows. But despite this, I desire to taste of my loneliness—I close my eyes and attempt to shut myself off, only now I see a carefully measured, carefully demarcated area, circled off and divided up by stones, markers, fences, and national flags; and then the picture is gone, I see nothing, hear nothing, neither the stillness of space nor the rumbling of celestial bodies as they roll across the horizon; I see the moon, this thing that was once—not long ago at all—hot, soft, boiling, and bubbling, but is now congealed and frozen, blisters scarring its contorted face, warty and notched, frozen in space and time, left standing without a sound, without an echo even, ready to be populated, to be defiled, a dead satellite—

or I see a half moon, partially hidden in shadow but recognizable as a sphere nonetheless, a cold, glowing balloon—no, not that, a rounded piece of hardened cheese, splotched and moldy—

but enough of this. The moon is but a point of departure for me—I want to expand, go elsewhere, explore places even further removed, although the farthest reaches will forever remain firmly out of my grasp, and not just mine—even the world's largest telescope would not be able to achieve such distance. For in the end it all comes down to the infinite continuation of the question—never will there be an absolute origin, and never will we find primordial matter. My telescope magnifies up to sixty times, which is not strong; but even if it were stronger, it would never be able to show me what I wish to see, for what I wish to see is nothing.

By "nothing," I do not mean that ever-so-fashionable something referred to as nothing, the so-called "absolute nothing," full of unbearable pathos, the undeterminable, malleable nothing of the philosophers, topic of lifeless conversations at round tables held in sound-dead, windowless rooms, stretched, bloated to its breaking point, a balloon of nothing, which is only called "nothing" because nothing better fits, the nothingness, the non-being of the being, whose workings concern nobody but those who work them—no: I mean the geographic, or better yet the cosmographic nothing, the empty space between the clusters, the masses, the groups of something, of much, of too much, the invisible between the visible, the hole in the sky, the tunnel in the heavens bored by my longing, my desire, like Celestina's desire for God, desire for a place where there is nothing, where there can be nothing, and where nothing ever was, this is what drives me upward, why my body grows roots at this very spot, roots that are older than those of the instrument in front of me, as old as the first stargazer. Galileo, Copernicus, Kepler are my older—and yes, smarter—brothers, who knew how to interpret what they saw, and who wished to share it—yes, brothers—for them, as for me, nothing is the empty space through which one gazes at something; nothing is between, and nothing more.

This is the nothing I am looking for. I look for it at different times of year and different times of night, at different spots in the heavens. This is the nothing I have been looking for ever since I came here, and sometimes I ask myself if my uncle had been looking for it as well, with this very same telescope. Did he too—this I would like to know—did he too search for the place where the heavens of picture books and legends lose their way, where the stars no longer have beautiful names, for the place where no captain, floundering between Scylla and Charybdis, has ever managed to regain orientation, where our twinkling companions dwindle and where chariots of fire do not climb, a place upon which Phaethon has never laid eyes, but where Icarus longs to ascend, a place avoided by suns and their systems, or at least the well-known ones? Perhaps my uncle had been searching for nothing, but then again perhaps not—it didn't really seem like him. But if he had been looking for nothing, he certainly would not have been able to find it with any greater accuracy or frequency than I'm able to now, or at least: than I was able to before I discovered how to limit my scope, at least by a little. For as much as I tinkered with the cranks and the knobs, adjusting the instrument millimeter by millimeter, there remained a single, fixed star right at the edge of my field of vision, an offshoot, perhaps, of a nearby galaxy, or the final point of a popular constellation. And when I turned the knob again, ever so slightly, in attempt to rid myself of this irritating fleck, a planet would appear on the other side, or the last wisps of a diffuse nebula, a planetary nebula even, would float by on the icy drafts of night air, sending chills through my body. Instead of a glow, I wanted a blue-ish black—the twinkling was making me dizzy. A quarter-turn upward got rid of the star, but replaced it with the fringes of an open cluster above, or perhaps a globular cluster; I did not find nothing, in fact I found nothing of nothing, and after a while I began to grow weary in my efforts.

At the zenith of my ignorance and self-deception, I even tried constructing a disc out of cardboard, from which I then cut a smaller, concentric circle, whose circumference was precisely the same as the circumference of the telescope's inner objective lens. I then unscrewed the metal casing, placed the disc directly onto the lens, and tightened the casing again. Doing so, I thought, would effectively shrink the radius of the objective lens, thus yielding a correspondingly smaller field of vision, which, in turn, would focus my gaze, forcing my eyes to penetrate farther forward instead of roaming from side to side. This is what I thought, at least, but is not at all what happened: as I placed my eye on the eyepiece once again I was greeted by the same glittering and twinkling as before, only slightly darker this time; but this was not at all the darkness for which I yearned.

The next step was to replace the eyepiece with one that was narrower but stronger. While doing so did serve to cut out some of the unwelcome peripheral interference, it also brought new problems into focus, nameless mazes of glowing orbs, interspersed with star dust—a new layer of light shone forth from behind the darkness, even if only dimly. But that's just it—it's all the same, I know too much now: wherever there appears to be darkness, I know that there is actually none, for true darkness does not exist. Behind the blackness that meets my eye are entire galaxies, giant solar systems, waiting to be uncovered by more powerful telescopes—but nowhere, not here, not there, is the nothing for which I am searching, the nothing about which I dream. Instead, there is just another something, visible, measureable, and eternally present. But what do they really prove, these sightings, these measurements, whom do they help? In actuality, they prove nothing, save for what we already know: that everything repeats itself.

But despite all of this, there are times—early in the summer, for instance—when, at just the right moment and just the right place, with just the slightest measure of self-deception, which I always exaggerate, I feel myself leaping into the darkness, pushing off from the moon and leaving the satellites and the other moons behind, deeper and deeper into space, into the darkness, the planet Earth fading farther and farther into the distance, a lifeless sphere overrun with parasites, its gravity gone, its energy spent; I can feel the heat of its core leaving my body, the magnetic pull lessening, I am lighter now, I am flying, drifting past the droning and whirring of other Earths and other planets, past hot suns, cold moons, through ever-shifting light. I graze against a crusty surface and plunge through a sea of fog, up and over the northern star fields; out here there's no trace of Creation, all of this had been in existence long before people started cooking up gods (who, after enough simmering, were eventually reduced to God). I slip away in the direction of a hole, a gap in the starry mesh on the far side of the Milky Way, continuing on in the direction of a promise, passing Iota Draconis to the north, while Theta and the twin stars Iota and Kappa, inhabitants of Boötes, float by to the south; I am passing everything, striking out into unending vastness, farther, and farther still, past the arc of Corona Borealis and the arms of Hercules, which will not earn its name until many millions of years later, for I am plunging deep into the unending past, now no different from the unending future, drawn by my longing to be nowhere, where there are no stars and is no light, where there is nothing, and where nothing is forgotten because nothing is remembered, where night is, where nothing is, nothing. There—

and here I stand, in my nightshirt and robe, arms hanging at my sides and an empty bottle in my hand. Tonight I will not look through the telescope. I think the sky is cloudy anyhow. There is a new weather system blowing in. I can feel it in my eyes and in my limbs. The fog bank is advancing, the edge of the front, while the last remnants of summer are swept away, leaving no trace. When will I sleep in my summer bed again?

I turn off the light, leave the room, lock the door, and step back out into the hallway.

Hamlet's father has disappeared, dissipated—in his place stands an accusation, but I refuse to accept it and it too evaporates, leaving a plume of mist and a few scraps of sound behind. I can still hear his calls to action, his challenges, as they trail off into the night, but I pay him no heed, no, not I.

Submitting to the whims of a rising darkness within me, I climb the stairs to the second floor: I wish to spy on objects in the night, to catch them in the midst of their unlit, unseen lives. I feel an urge to cast a sudden beam of light onto Jean Gaspard's painting, so that perhaps, before the canvas is once again engulfed in blackness, I will catch a fleeting glimpse of its subject; or to run my hands over the plumage of an extinct bird in the hopes that it will snap back,

no: I will visit my summer bed and think of warm nights, of dreadful nights—

I open the door, step into the room, and turn on the light—there it stands, right in the middle of the room, the room that belongs entirely to it, so large that seven people could sleep comfortably side by side—their limbs stretched out, twitching and thrashing in the throes of fitful dreams—without getting in each other's way, unless, of course, that is what they wished to do, although it is much more likely that what they wished to do was wake up.

Since I've owned it, however, it has never held seven sleepers at once; only I sleep in it—or rather, lie sleeplessly in it—and only in summer.

I sleep whenever I find myself able to, reveling in the bliss of being lost—I like to lie diagonally and stretch myself out as far as I can, knowing that, try as I might, I will never reach a corner; I am engulfed by my bed and its soft, cool linen.

It's not the largest bed I have ever seen, though. In London, in the Victoria and Albert Museum, there is a larger one. It is called "The Great Bed of Ware," which one would do well to distinguish from "The Big" or "The Large Bed of Ware." The full force of the word "great" in this context cannot be derived from any physical dimensions, but will only be felt upon con- templation of the piece's inner splendor, its importance in the narrative of a historical epoch, the slumberous past to which it bore witness. The town of Ware is located in the county of

Hertfordshire, where today one can still find a gothic cathedral, three brickyards, and a malt house, but the tavern in which this bed once stood, so broad, so welcoming, its four lathed posts like solid oak columns, bearing the weight of the canopy above, the crossbeams adorned with intricate carvings and decorative inlays, the multiple shades of wood stain like markers in time— the tavern is gone; in its place there is probably some hotel with unspeakable food. Hospitality has spread where fates used to meet, passing each other by in silent slumber.

The Great Bed of Ware is from the seventeenth century, and back then it would have regularly held up to twelve people at once. My bed, on the other hand, only ever held seven. I acquired it from a private seller—just the frame, of course: no mattress, no canopy, no drapes, and no linens. He was in the process of getting rid of some of his more "unwieldy items," I suppose you might say; this was a person who fell in love easily with details, who could lose himself for hours while studying an eyebrow, or a royal ornament, a person who made frequent use of a magnifying glass. As far as my bed is concerned, he was happy to have it gone, for it, you see, is devoid of detail, utterly unornamented, shamelessly so, in fact. It is also considerably cruder than The Bed of Ware: its wood boasts neither stain nor engraving, its breadth is entirely utilitarian. Absent is the desire to lull the guest into peaceful slumber through exaggerated aesthetics—what this bed offers is sleep, the purest and most natural of all enticements.

It comes from the Midland county of Cheshire, from a city known as Skye, and dates back farther than the Bed of Ware— to the early sixteenth century, to be exact. Until the Plague struck in 1522, it had also resided in an inn of sorts, but a simpler one than that of the Bed of Ware, one that primarily housed travelers on foot, weary wanderers with neither luck nor fortune.

As I mentioned earlier, it offered seven sleeping places—perhaps not every night, but during the great pilgrimages, market gatherings, or other such events, it would consistently fill to capacity, and it was not at all unusual for guests to be turned away. And those who did make it found themselves sleeping side by side with people they very often didn't know—with the exception of the married couples, of course—people they would later encounter only by sheer coincidence, at the dinner table, perhaps, or elsewhere in the inn, or if not, then certainly the following night when they were back under the same set of sheets. Then again it also happened that those sleeping on the outer edges never even saw the occupants of the other side: by the time one of them came to bed, the other may already have been asleep, and in the morning it was similarly common for one to vacate the room far earlier than the other. Sometimes, in the summer, I imagine that I am the last of the seven sleepers—on either side of me are the imprints of three other destinies, which despite their proximity to my own, never once touched it. I imagine that I am one of the last seven sleepers—a disgraced monk, perhaps, or a weary soldier, a German nobleman whose disgust with the world led him blindly stumbling into this room, or a miller with a full stomach.

This is where I spend my summer nights, lying in the bed that once offered places for seven, but in which seven have not slept for a long time, not since that night in late spring, or shall we say early summer, of the year 1522—that was the last time seven people slept here—

the first to arrive was a man, maybe a monk, in the early evening. He was lanky and thin save for his large, broad feet, which had been hardened from miles of barefoot travel on the path of self-abnegation. He was quite weary upon reaching the inn that housed my bed, for he had been traveling for weeks without rest, all the way from St. Gallen—he was headed for Ireland. Upon arrival, he made his way into the dining area and assembled for himself a hodgepodge of leftover food, which the innkeeper was more than happy to provide free of charge in the hopes that doing so would secure her a place in the afterlife, to which she—for some reason or another—did not feel entitled otherwise. The monk ate quickly, muttered a quick prayer, attended to his other very scant needs, and then headed upstairs to the bedroom where the bed was waiting. He removed his scapular and cincture—while at the very same moment another wanderer, a female this time, was making her way through the night to the inn's door—but kept his cowl on and wound the rosary even tighter around his wrist so that it would continue to pray for him as he slept. He lifted the covers and climbed into the bed, positioning himself at the outermost edge, for he wanted to be the first to rise in the morning—this wasn't in an effort to save himself from embarrassment of some sort (embarrassment didn't even exist back then) but merely because he had a very long way ahead. The thought of temptation didn't even cross his mind.

Was the moon shining?

Yes—or perhaps we should say it wasn't shining yet, for it was still making its ascent into the night sky—a three-quarters moon, I believe. Its light had not yet reached the window behind which the monk was lying in bed, but it did cast a long shadow from the feet of the second guest, who, as the monk was undressing, reached the inn's door, and as he lay down, stepped inside, shedding the moon's shadows from her body in the process. She was a woman who had seen better nights and cringed at the thought of seeing worse, although she never would—a courtesan, I'll call her Anne. Anne was aging, and had fallen from the graces of her most recent patron, the old Duke of Northumberland—if this was still his title—who had, rather suddenly, developed a taste for the untouched hymen of his serfs' underage daughters and elected to reinstate the *jus primae noctis*—but that's another story, and probably not a very good one.

Anne was traveling from the grand estates of the north to the

gutters of the south, to London or perhaps somewhere in France.
Her hopes were modest, but not yet abandoned—after all, she
was still quite good-looking, quite lush. But it was beneath her
lusciousness that things had started to change: her skin was no
longer drawn taut over the undulating landscape of her feminine
figure, but peppered with creases and wrinkles, and her silken
garments had begun to fade while the velvet ones had become
shiny and threadbare. As the monk slid under the covers and
wrapped the rosary around his hands for one final, and I mean
final, prayer—I now know what I'm getting at—Anne was in
the process of draining a pitcher of beer with the innkeeper,
telling stories while the moon's shadows grew shorter—one of
which may well have landed on a married couple, a miller and
his wife, trudging along the dusty road, still quite far from the
inn, but getting nearer and nearer with every step—in the crass
vernacular of the time, she was telling stories about the giant,
mirror-lined rooms she had left behind forever. The innkeeper
listened in silence, taking special pains not to mention the bed's
first occupant, who was quite antithetical to the woman sitting
across from her now, the man whose covered body had just been
touched by the first thin streak, the first sliver, of moonlight
from the bedroom window. Despite the fact that he was accustomed to sleeping arrangements that were much different and—
truth be told—much worse than those presented by his current
situation, the monk could not rid his mind of ominous thoughts.
While Anne ravenously dismembered a squab downstairs, suck-
ing on her fingers after every bite, he concentrated on shepherd-
ing his thoughts back to the middle of the road—from where
they had strayed in their nightly wanderings—the road that led
straight to God, averting his mind's eye from all branches and
side paths, although he rarely noticed these anyway. And downstairs sat the innkeeper, sat Anne, cracking, slurping, swallowing, licking her lips, and pouring another beer to wash the meal
down—and upstairs lay the monk, weary from his efforts, while
the wanderers continued their journey outside, presided over by

the night, the moon climbing ever higher in the sky, illuminating an even larger swath of the bed where the monk was falling asleep. Down below, Anne wiped her mouth on her forearm, gathered her skirts, wished the innkeeper a good night, and slowly began climbing the stairs to the bedroom. The moon did not shine on the stairs, nor did it shine into the kitchen, where the innkeeper had returned to prepare a meal—the last meal—for the guests that had not yet arrived. It did, however, shine rather brightly upon the miller and his wife, who were drawing nearer and nearer to the inn's front door, while missing entirely—or mostly, at least—the man who had just reached it (here enters the fugue's third voice), a young soldier returning from—what battle?—returning from the Siege of Padua, the same siege in which Frau Marthe Schwerdtlein's husband met his end and Duke Maximilian of Bavaria was dealt an honorable sword wound. He is no older than nineteen, but during the last several days his body has aged drastically, wasting away to the point where he barely casts a shadow, despite the fact that he is in plain view of the moon. What the moon can't see are Anne on the staircase and the innkeeper in the kitchen, but no matter, there is still the question of the monk upstairs. A lone moonbeam is now streaming through the bedroom window, and with it comes a dream that alights on the sleeping figure and flutters in his ear. It is an innocent dream, albeit somewhat less innocent by today's standards; little by little it creeps into his body and begins to take hold—how is the fugue progressing? Anne upstairs, the soldier at the front door, the miller and his wife drawing nearer, another wanderer still quite far off, and another couple even farther, the dream in the monk, the monk in the bed, the moon in the sky, and Anne begins to undress, laying her hennin, veil, collar, and stomacher to the side, followed by her gown, her corset, her overdress, and her slip, peeling away layers until there are none left, until she stands there as God made her, even if not how he created her: stark naked and hopeful for a night of fruitful adventures; the only item she does not remove is the golden chain around her neck, from which hangs an ivory figurine of the Redeemer—this she keeps on, but not on account of any faith or belief she still harbors, no; although he did play a large part in her rigorous and disciplined upbringing, these times have long since passed; she has kept the necklace all these years because it is an item of great worth and may very well prove useful during the uncertain times ahead. Standing there in her nakedness, her eyes eventually come to rest on the scapular and cingulum, veiled in the blackness of the dark room, while the moon shines bright on the dust-coated doublet worn by the soldier, who is at this very moment entering the inn while death continues to eat away at his body; the moon does not shine on death, however—of the billions of objects available to it, it chooses instead to cast its beams on the miller and his wife, who are now very close to the inn, driven by the desire for a good meal, as well as the other wanderer, who has just reached the city gate, and the second pair, who are still quite far off; it shines on Anne's astonishment, but not the hand she uses to cross herself, for she doesn't cross herself; her eyes scan the bed, my summer bed, for the garments' owner, and find him at the end of a slanted moonbeam; what she does not see is the devil lurking behind her in the dark, the devil that smiles and makes her smile; the moon continues to shine on the pious sleeper's dream, whose contents form the contrapuntal opposite of the scene unfolding before him, or maybe they don't. The soldier is no longer bathed in moonlight, for he has now entered the inn and is standing before the innkeeper. The moon has ascended higher into the sky, and casts a shortened shadow over the miller and his wife as they approach the inn, as well as an equally short one over the lone traveler—a barber surgeon, by the way—who has now passed through the city gates; it casts shadows over the other pair as well, two men this time, still difficult to recognize—I haven't yet made up my mind about them—two men who still haven't reached the gates, but whose paths will come to an end in this very bed—come to an end, I'm afraid I've given away the ending. The miller and his wife at the door, the barber surgeon in the moonlight, the dream in the monk, the monk in the bed, Anne in the bed, the soldier in the inn, the innkeeper with the soldier—she watches as he gropes his way forward, pale and shaky, with no other wish than to make it to bed, while she gropes him with her eyes—to her he is pale and shaky and handsome—and attempts to lure him into her own bed before he collapses into the giant one upstairs with the others; she shows him everything that she has to offer, while hinting at a few other services she has borrowed from Anne's vast trove of stories, but the soldier doesn't listen, for he is barely even aware of his surroundings, to say nothing of good looks and intriguing promises; each of her advances is met with mute resistance, the shaking of a head; he does not hunger for her flesh, he doesn't hunger for anything; he is thirsty—not for ale, however, but for water, water, and he empties an entire jug in giant, painful gulps as the moon rises higher into the night sky, but not high enough, shining on the earth, on England, on the county, on the city, on the inn, on the miller and his wife standing in front of it; perhaps they're on their way back from the reading of a will and are satisfied with their inheritance, satisfied with the world and the possessions it consists of; its slanted beams shine on the lone traveler in the night, whose every step brings him closer and closer to the inn—a barber surgeon, as I mentioned, and a rather destitute one at that; somewhere in life he went astray, and it has been quite a while since he has owned his own bathhouse—all in all a dishonest man; they shine on the other pair who have now reached the city gates, an elderly German nobleman in the later stages of degeneration accompanied by a handsome young lad with white teeth and a lute slung across his back; they have decided not to travel any farther tonight, although they didn't really have a destination to begin with—it has been a long time since the nobleman has felt even the slightest interest in having a destination to strive for; in all honesty, this is something he never felt, but that would be yet another story—a good one this time.

Onward: the moon has now risen high into the sky, but still only illuminates a small part of the bed on which I am sitting right now; the bed on whose edge Anne, stark naked save for the golden chain with the Redeemer figurine, sits down and lifts the covers back; where the man of God is already lying, his innocence fading; beginning at his ankles, she lightly runs her fingers up his legs, lifting his robe as if it were a sheath, the contents of which are not terribly surprising in and of themselves but which recoil in surprise at the woman's touch—the moonlight shines in patches on the body of the sleeping monk, now only half sleeping as her hand continues its journey up his leg, not yet aware of his companion's identity, or her intentions; and then comes a state of alertness he has never before experienced, a forbidden awakening, a realization of her identity but an inability to believe it, and the moon shines bright on his disbelief, on the graceful dancing of Anne's practiced fingers; but it does not shine on the soldier making his way through the inn's darkened corridor; his gums dry and his throat on fire, he uses the last of his strength to grasp the railing and pull himself, hand over hand, up the stairs to the second floor while the innkeeper stares ruefully from below; nor does it shine on the miller and his wife, who at this very moment have stepped through the front door, laden with all manner of transportable goods, shrouded in an opulent haze—it doesn't shine on the innkeeper either, who has withdrawn her gaze from the object of her lust and directed it toward the newcomers, a fresh wave of hope welling up inside of her as she eyes the contents of their bulging sack; the moonlight shines almost vertically on the barber surgeon, who is now not far at all, a miserable peddler of indulgences, a blood sucker with a locked-up vendor's tray, a wad of paper slips in his clenched fist, an enema syringe in his pack, and a taste for ale and vice on his tongue; it shines on the other pair as well, on the nobleman and his wasting countenance, his dwindling wealth, his lost possessions—there isn't even a horse to shine on; the only things he owns anymore are right there with him: a small rucksack on his shoulder, a sagging purse against his hip, and the young lad with the lute on his back (as well as a few other qualities equally fitting to the night). The moon shines on as if nothing terrible is about to happen, shines on Anne as her hand finally reaches its goal, poised at the middle point of the monk's body as if about to pick a flower from the very base of its stem; and then, with a single, languid heave of her soft body, she swings the entirety of her mortal self over this middle point, lowering herself down like a rider into a saddle and shifting her weight until she is securely mounted—the moon does not shine on the monk anymore, for its path is blocked by the figure perched on top of him; at the top of his lungs, he screams "Satanas!" and then mumbles it again, the consonants softer this time, almost dying on his breath, and then whispers it so that only the vowels are audible, his lips freezing around a final *s* as the moon, almost at its zenith, moves closer and closer to the corner from which the soldier laboriously staggers into the room's dark interior, as oblivious to the writhing paleness on the other side of the bed as he is to the screams that fade into the choppy air. The kitchen is brightened somewhat by the fire in the stove, which keeps the innkeeper company as she cuts meat and fills pitchers; a couple of tallow candles cast a dim, flickering light into the dining room, where the miller and his wife eagerly await their imminent meal; the moon shines brightly on the barber surgeon as he knocks on the inn's front door; the golden chain glistens as the crucifix bobs up and down before the monk's eyes, catching the light that reflects from its owner's white skin while the limb that binds the monk to his mortal sin remains black, enveloped in primal darkness; the moon shines brightly on the nobleman as well, on whose back many countries' moons have shone over the years, always on the move, always searching (he's a German) for the absolute, which he will soon find—I've arranged it for him; the moonlight also falls on the nobleman's companion, the undeserving object of his affection, a handsome lad with arched eyebrows but unsteady eyes, with murder in his heart and a lute on his back—the innkeeper's silhouette is only partially lit by the tallow candles as she walks into the dining room carrying food for her guests—but the faces of the miller and his wife are fully aglow as they reach for the pitchers of ale and pile their plates high with hearty fare; the barber surgeon stands before the door and knocks as the beams of light stream down upon him, and for a moment the innkeeper is moonlit as well—standing at the window, she peers out into the night and asks for the stranger's identity; his answer floats back through the moonlight: "I'm a barber surgeon." "We don't need anything," she responds to the glowing man, "we're all healthy here." Peering back at the gleaming face in the window, he replies that he is not here in his capacity as barber surgeon, or as a peddler, a leech, or a distributor of indulgences. No, tonight he has come as a paying guest in search of a hot meal and a place to sleep. Unimpeded by clouds, the light streams down through the night sky onto the horror that continues to spread through its carrier while the monk remains shrouded in shadow, sinking deeper and deeper into the blessed void of forgetting, his thoughts receding like black clouds in the distance, and with them the realization that he has eternally fallen from grace—but what even is eternity anyhow? At any rate, his earthly days will soon be at an end, and at this very moment they are making his bed in Hell. Sitting in the darkness, the soldier, bearer of the others' gruesome fate, forces his cramping fingers to loosen his boots and unbutton his shirt while the innkeeper opens the front door, leading the barber surgeon out of the moonlight. But horrors such as this spread with equal rapidity through darkness and light, and if the monk, for instance, had had any idea of what would soon befall him, he would have prayed to the ivory Jesus bouncing up and down in front of him; but he remains oblivious. No matter: if not this

one then surely another, slower death—for the woman currently
straddling him has been infected with the French variant, which
she caught from her former lover, the Duke of Northumberland,
who is at this very moment passing it on to some serf's daughter;
it was given to him by his wife, and to her from King Henry III,
who brought it from France when it was still rather uncommon.

Good: all of the voices have now entered and the exposition has
drawn to a close. Now we continue. It is a little after midnight
when the moon finally reaches its zenith in the sky, at which
point it no longer shines upon the bed—and it is in this fresh
darkness that our tragedy's second act unfolds. In the case of
the monk, this term can be interpreted quite literally: it really
is the second act of his life. In a violent effort to lose himself
in the oblivion of the moment, or perhaps just to plumb the
depths of his sinful nature, he forces the courtesan onto her
back and thrusts himself into farthest reaches of her infectious
depth, while she, lying there at the mercy of her lanky bedmate,
begins to regret her decision as it dawns on her that this is not
the business transaction she had thought it to be. In the middle
of the darkened bed lies the soldier, clinging to the last shards
of consciousness, his eyes glazed and his fever rising, while the
others continue to linger in the dining room. The miller and his
wife are engrossed in their meal—but what are they eating? Let's
say pork shank boiled with pepper and millet, accompanied by
rhubarb, saffron, and thyme; that sounds like the proper degree
of fat-laden indulgence. And of course, plenty of ale and wine
to drink. On the other end of the table, next to his murderous,
boyish companion, sits the German, his back locked upright,
his eyes staring into the emptiness in front of him, in full expectation and grim acceptance of each humiliation wrought upon
his name, his doubts confirmed and his hopelessness cemented
by the pitiful worth of the world and the objects that populate
it. Before him stands a jug of wine, with whose help he hopes to
endure the night ahead, in an unfamiliar bed among unfamiliar

guests, by slipping peacefully into a drunken slumber. His companion, on the other hand, seems to display a certain interest in
the present company, even if only out of fascination with some
of the pieces of jewelry that glint from between the breasts of the
miller's wife, who casts increasingly frequent and lustful glances
in his direction, and whose glances he returns. The kitchen is
only partially illuminated as the innkeeper refreshes the jugs and
pitchers for her guests and as the barber surgeon steps in to join
her, offering, among other things, to let her blood free of charge
if she will only look the other way and allow him to conduct his
business freely among the other guests. The moonlight is shining
diagonally again as the monk finally withdraws from Anne,
slipping out of her as if from a hollowed pear; his intention is
to escape under the cover of sleep as quickly as possible, where
he will live out the remainder of his shameful days shrouded in
dreams—perhaps his body will create a new spirit; the moon is
lower still—on the other side of the bed now—as Anne sits up
and sighs, filled with regret about an act of good will carried out
for naught; shivering, she ducks out of the light and puts on her
slip; as her gaze wanders around the room, she catches sight of
the soldier with the glazed eyes lying in the middle of the bed;
she studies him calculatingly. But the soldier takes no notice:
he has long since sunken into a feverish delirium and begun his
journey into the other realm, bound to the earth by nothing but
a few lingering moments of excruciating pain.

And what binds me to this earth?

Onward, onward, transposition, new theme: the development
of the night's horrors has taken a steep upward curve, the moon
is setting now, and by this point has nearly reached the edge of
the opposite horizon; it shines through the bedroom window
once again, this time illuminating the entire bed, my bed, whose
empty space is now fully occupied by slumbering bodies, bathed
in the merciless light of the night's most radiant orb. The monk,

who will be spared a rude and terrifying awakening, sleeps the
deepest of them all, while Anne, having regained consciousness a few moments earlier, in an effort to put some distance
between herself and her earlier conquest, slides gingerly in the
direction of the soldier, taking great pains not to awaken him
before she has regained full command of her facilities. Save for
the recurring bouts of shaking, teeth chattering, and quivering
gasps, the soldier continues to lie motionless in the middle of
the bed. The other guests have made their way to the sleeping quarters as well and begin to undress along the edges of
the bedroom—this doesn't happen all at once, however, but in
overlapping stages, and the empty places on the mattress fill in
a choreographed silence. Only one of them is forced to crawl
along the foot of the bed to reach his desired spot, and that is
the miller—for he has now caught sight of Anne, and the supple locks of unbraided hair that fall around her shoulders; as he
watches her body snaking under the covers toward the soldier,
the promise of a late-night adventure looms large in his racing
mind; his choice to climb is voluntary, for only by doing so will
he be able to put some distance between himself and his wife,
not to mention the other unidentifiable figure (the soldier), and
get closer to the object of his lust—the empty space between her
and the monk is simply too small for a pair. The miller's wife,
however, is similarly uninterested in this spot, for she is hot on
the trail of the nobleman's handsome traveling companion and
will do anything to lie at his side (with the hope, of course, that
she won't remain at his side for very long); her only worry is that
the lad's master will prove an impasse, jealously forcing himself between them and pushing the boy to the edge. In reality,
though, such behavior is the farthest thing from the nobleman's
mind. Wishing nothing more than to avoid any and all contact
with the other sleepers—save for the lad, of course, with whom
he is almost constantly in contact—he positions himself at the
edge of the bed, with his companion at his side, granting the
miller's wife the place she desires; she lies down between the

young man and the soldier, whom she barely even notices. And there they are: seven sleepers, none of them actually sleeping, save for the man of God. One of them is dying, and the others wait patiently for their bedmates to drift off so that their love-making can commence.

Where is the barber surgeon? The barber surgeon, the poor bastard, he's still downstairs with the innkeeper. I haven't yet decided what he's doing down there—perhaps he's preparing her a beauty ointment, buying away her sins in exchange for indulgences, letting her blood, or lying with her in bed; perhaps he's doing all of these things at once, a vicious circle of transgression and compensation; but I'll leave this scene where it is, in the dark—let us return now to the theme at hand, to the main key, the potential past of my summer bed, where the sinking moon shines on the merciless advance of horror. It is still on the march, however, and has yet to descend upon its unsuspecting victims: the nobleman still clings to the young lad beside him, who reaches for the miller's wife, who reaches for him, while the miller reaches for Anne, and Anne for the soldier, and the monk continues to sleep and the soldier continues to die; temporarily free from the prying moonlight, hands grope under the covers, breath quickens, legs entangle, and bodies silently begin to roll; soon the entire bed is undulating, forming waves of hills and valleys, the intermittent moonbeams casting fleeting shadows against the walls—the bed has come alive, but for the last time; all of a sudden, the occupants freeze, waiting with bated breath for the final move, hungrily anticipating the triumphant thrust; all except for the monk, that is—he isn't waiting for anything; he isn't really sleeping anymore either, nor will he ever wake; he is lying at the edge of a gaping abyss that has opened up before him, staring, paralyzed, into the pit of Hell. The soldier has also remained still, for he has now given up the fight with death and surrendered himself as a willing victim; coated in a greasy layer of sweat, gums swollen, and black boils sprinkled across

his loins; from time to time a hoarse, rattling gasp can be heard
scraping through his throat, temporarily jolting the others out
of the predatory trance in which they pursue their desires; and
then there is silence again, relaxation; as the moon sinks even
lower, Anne, sensing the speed at which her window of opportunity is closing, slides closer to the soldier, much closer, with the
miller in hot pursuit; he too feels that the time for action is now,
despite the gradually widening gap between him and the retreat-
ing courtesan; but just as he is about to lunge, he is suddenly
overcome with fatigue, at the same time as the nobleman, who,
as the lust drains from his body, lets go of the boy at his side
and allows the spinning darkness to wash over him; thinking
that his master has finally fallen asleep, the boy crawls on top of
the miller's wife, crouching over her like an animal thirsting for
blood—but even he feels his strength fading; as she lies on her
back, hot from anticipation of the youthful body sliding deeper
and deeper between her legs, the miller's wife suddenly feels a
different kind of feverish heat, which Anne feels as well, accompanied by a growing weakness; but she persists nonetheless: she
wants the soldier, wants to take him for herself, softly, gently;
she lifts the covers and reaches for his body as the setting moon
casts horizontal beams of light on her hair and her neck; but it
does not shine on the others anymore—the miller, the monk,
the miller's wife, the boy, the nobleman, and the soldier are
engulfed in blackness, lying on the bed as if they had just fallen
down, their resolve defeated, their lust quickly fading; a feeling
of nausea begins to spread through the miller's innards, forcing
him to abandon the pursuit of his voluptuous prey and sink
into the mattress; the monk is now awake, his tormented spirit
numbed by the weight of an aching body, that of the miller's
wife, whose heavy breaths are no longer the result of lust, but
instead a symptom of the pain taking hold of her; she lets go of
the boy, and the boy of her as he falls back into place next to the
nobleman, who turns his back and rolls farther toward the edge
of the bed; they are all weak now, and waves of heat and cold

take turns crashing against the bed, bringing fresh bouts of pain and teeth chattering with them; all action has subsided now, and a feverish dusk envelops the room: apathy; rattling, labored breaths; and in between, silence—until there comes a scream, whose piercing shrillness cuts through their ears but does not wake them, does not lift the fog that shrouds their senses; it comes from Anne, the only one who is still partially upright and still moving. The miller, the miller's wife, the nobleman, and the boy each cast her a lifeless glance, eight eyes stare detachedly at her horror-stricken face and follow her gaze downward:

to the vertical pillar, pale white in the light of the sinking moon, that, until recently, had been the living symbol of soldier's manhood; its current stiffness is not the result of desire, but instead a sign of rigor mortis, jutting forth from the putrid landscape of his bloated body, a cross without a crossbar, a hideous memento mori erected above a battlefield upon which war still rages—

and everything else lies in darkness. It becomes even quieter in the room; the courtesan's choking sobs gradually subside and she lowers herself down onto the bed next to the soldier, the terror in her eyes much dimmer now—dying amongst the dying, in my bed; and from this bed, from the seven bodies under its loosened covers, the Plague spreads outward in a cloud, enveloping first the canopy and then filling the entire room, poisoning its air, before seeping through the cracks into the city outside, where it continues to spread, slowly but surely engulfing the entire country in its toxic fog; though it has since died out, the Bubonic Plague was, during its heyday, the blackest, hardest, foulest, and fastest variant of the Black Death, knowing no mercy and granting its victims no favors, nothing, not even a moment to reflect, and not even a second of euphoric ecstasy. As the last convulsions of agony fade, so does the consciousness, which is replaced by rigor mortis—no time for penitence and no space for insight. Fermata. End of the fugue.

But not the end of the story. As the sky turns from black to gray in the early hours of the morning, the innkeeper enters the bedroom to awaken the alleged sleepers. But she awakens nobody, for nobody is sleeping. Nobody is dead either, save for the soldier—they are all lying there, side by side, gasping their final breaths, too weak to move or to speak, their bodies bloated, acutely aware of their every limb, of every inch of their fading physicality, but of nothing more; they are all the same now, the field is level, no more sin, no hope, no crime, no inheritance, no fear. Bedded deep in apathy, none of them know what they are suffering from, who they even were before they began suffering, or that their suffering is close to being at an end. And none of them pay any heed to the innkeeper and the barber surgeon as they rob them of their very last possessions—not only the various articles of clothing scattered around the room, but the items on their persons as well. Carefully lifting heads and bodies, the innkeeper and the barber surgeon reach for the pouches of money stowed under nightgowns and in pillowcases, and slip rings from fingers; there is nobody to stop them—Anne doesn't make a sound, doesn't even open her eyes as the innkeeper rips the golden chain with the ivory figurine from her neck; she feels neither pain nor loss—

it's only the monk who makes one final miserable attempt at defense as they slip the rosary, the only possession he ever had, from around his wrists; his god, not the god of the priests, but the god of the sinners, has given him the strength for one last protest: as the barber surgeon pries the beaded chain from his clenched fist, the monk lets forth a final, guttural scream—the summation of all of the screams through all of the centuries— over his pain and under his pain he can still feel the deep eternity of his damnation,

but shortly thereafter he feels nothing; in fact, it's unlikely that any of them felt anything as their bodies slammed against the rocks and sunk into the icy cold water as the innkeeper and the barber surgeon threw them one by one into the river. And as the innkeeper and the barber surgeon talked about their future together, the sleepers' corpses were whisked downriver, to the south, and as the innkeeper and the barber surgeon climbed back into bed, drained from the morning's activities, the Plague continued its journey down the river, swelling over its banks and drifting in clouds up the shore, spreading wider and wider. The innkeeper and the barber surgeon never stood up again, but rotted side by side in the innkeeper's bed as the Plague took hold of Wiltshire and Kent, where it met another Plague, this one traveling northward from Sussex, where the soldier had stopped to rest only a few evenings earlier, infecting a little girl who infected her family who infected the rest of the town, and so on and so forth. End of story. I'm getting up.

I lie in this bed during the summer nights, sleeping when I can, and if it is only faintly that I feel the presence of these last unfortunate sleepers coalesce with my own consciousness, it is perhaps because they never existed in the first place. What a shame. If they had lived, maybe they could have told me things, maybe I could have learned from them, if I were actually capable of learning, that is; certainly nothing from the young murderer with the lute, and nothing from the soldier either—though a positive hero in his innocence, he was only half alive when he lay down in this bed; no, nothing from them—

but perhaps something from somebody like Anne, the unabashed prostitute, who, though broken and abused, faces her inevitable demise with a cool assuredness, an indifference free of protest or accusation, for she knew and respected the order of the world—

and from this unusual German man, robbed of everything he owned, deeply mistrustful of the legitimacy of the law that granted him his power, searching for something, but not sure what, something he would only recognize after he had failed to find it, but no one would find it before it was too late to do any good,

and from the monk, the quiet and devoted wanderer who refused to commune with his fellow man until his final dying hour, when he perhaps communed too much, but still not enough to relinquish hope of redemption—

I could learn something from these people—even if only a little; and now I am growing tired, I think I'll go down to my winter bed now, I think I'll sleep.

But first I'll get the wine. My thirst for it is stronger now. I leave the bedroom, closing the door behind me, and start down the stairs—there he is again, the ghost; maybe he was lured closer by my story, hoping to gain some sort of insight from hearing it, but I pay him no heed; as I continue down the stairs I simply walk by him, passing through his gaze as if it weren't even there.

Eventually I make it to the kitchen, a vaulted room paneled with unvarnished and unstained wood, naturally colored and naturally dark, its age growing more and more apparent with time, to the point that I even start to feel younger when I enter; checkered curtains hang from the windows—a childhood kitchen— and the shelves are lined with earthen crocks filled with flour and sugar, and herb boxes infused with the lingering aromas of stonecrop, tarragon, and coriander, which have now melded into one non-descript scent of spice. The walls are lined with bulky kettles and unwieldy pans made from copper and brass and iron, the kind that nobody uses anymore, except for Celestina.

She handles such cookware quite naturally, and with an air of stubborn determination. Earlier on, but not for quite some time now, I used to bring her replacements, chrome plated, adjustable, and shiny, the newest in practical, timesaving patents whose

revolutionary effectiveness was written right there on the label:
what used to take hours would now be a matter of minutes;
but Celestina didn't so much as lay a finger on them; in fact,
she barely seemed to notice they were there—of course I now
understand that she was absolutely right to do so. What would
she have even done with the extra free time? Prayed? Drunk?
Tortured herself with the certainty that she would never make
it to Heaven's gates while painting a picture of her eternal damnation with its endless circles and levels? No, it's better like this,
better that she busy herself with cumbersome objects than allow
idleness to lead her astray. It was pure rationality that caused
her to breathe an inaudible sigh of disdain and clear away every
piece of equipment designed to make life easier; for her, the only
suitable tools are those that make life more burdensome, that
encourage mindless drudgery and hardening, but redemptive
toil, to be carried out over a lifetime for pennies on the hour in
the hopes that one day she may have saved up enough to buy her
way back to eternal salvation. But she fears that life may be too
short for such aspirations, and that, by the end, she won't have
endured enough of its relentlessly mounting torment.

    Now and again she would come and stand next to me in
the kitchen, passing me a newspaper clipping that I was to read
in her presence. It was always something about a housewife in
Lüneburg or Cremona who was using one of these new-fangled
devices when all of a sudden it exploded, causing her serious
and sometimes irreparable injury. I always pretended to read the
article in its entirety, summoning a look of serious introspection
and shaking my head as Celestina stood behind me. I hardly
dared to turn around, for I wanted at all costs to avoid the look
of accusation in her eyes, the look that condemned me as a
murderer—a murderer who was intent on doing her in as well
with the help of an elaborate and sinister contraption. But these
were also the moments from which our mutual allegiance to one
another was born, felt by both of us at the same time and in the
same measure, an accusation from one side met by the other's

realization, our loyalties feeling their way toward each other in the dark, turning into an alliance upon first meeting, fusing to form a bond that was inseparable, and yet still unrecognized. I would then hand the newspaper clipping back to her in silence, temporarily healed of my weakness, until, of course, I came upon a new gadget with even more impressive features, at which point the whole process began anew. Eventually I learned not to purchase such things, and gradually it became clear to me that any attempt to change Celestina, to convert her to anything that could be construed as "ungodly" was an exercise in utter futility, and would only drive her to more drinking and more praying—two activities of which only one is futile. Moreover, I was in absolutely no position to complain about her cooking— quite the contrary, actually: her culinary abilities are first-rate, although I have no idea where she acquired them—just another one of her secrets. One night, as I was rummaging through the kitchen drawers looking for a corkscrew, I found a notebook containing all of the newspaper clippings she had ever brought to me: a list of sins, a complete account of transgressions to be used against me on the Day of Reckoning. I left it where I found it, and when I looked again a short while later it was gone. I suspect she ended up destroying it out of shame for herself and her suspicions, and I am almost certain—no, quite certain—that today she would have no memory of it.

I walk into the kitchen but I do not turn on the light. There is a candle burning on the table. It is not enough light to fill the room, but it does make it so that various nearby objects are recognizable, while others are cast in dark, angular silhouettes against the walls. On either side of the candle, closer to the long edges of the table, stands a pair of wine glasses. One of the glasses is full, and the other half full, half empty. Behind the half glass sits Celestina, and behind the other there is no one, though from the way the chair has been pulled ever so slightly from the table it looks as if she has been expecting a second party.

What is certain is that I was not who she was expecting—I am able to glean this from the look she casts in my direction as I enter the room. There is no fear in her eyes; neither is there surprise. I am not yet able to interpret this look—the scene is not yet clear, the silent events have not yet unfolded; on top of that, Celestina's various glances have started to become quite similar to one another, their range has grown narrower, which means the mystery of who the full glass was intended for, and on whose account the chair was pulled from the table, will for the time being remain unsolved. And that's just as well. I enjoy the unexpected riddles of the night, its secret agendas—this is my element, I am playing my role. And at this point all I know for certain is that the time to involve myself has not yet arrived.

I was sleepy earlier; I hadn't slept at all, or if I had, only very little. But after this scene, whatever it's supposed to depict, however it's meant, when the stage goes dark and the action—which is escalating at this very moment, the tension rising, the zenith approaching—has finally come to an end, I will certainly sleep then, I know it. Now I am wide awake, tense with excitement; and then suddenly, whatever amount of sleep I have managed to accumulate is gone, the memory vanished, everything has disappeared,

except for Tynset. Tynset cannot be driven out—it remains there in the background, and suddenly has assumed a peculiar clarity, an expanding gray aridity one might normally associate with late autumn. I enjoy gazing upon it, back there where nothing moves, where there are neither trees nor shadows between the houses,

but here in the front there are other forces at play, like Celestina and the glasses of wine, and her gaze, which remains fixed on me as I approach the table, pull out the chair, and sit down silently across from her, behind the full glass of wine. I feel a great urge to drink it, but I wait. Celestina does nothing, says nothing; she simply stares at me in silence, without the slightest hint of astonishment, her eyes neither glazed nor fixed, staring at me just as she had been staring at the empty chair before I had entered the room. She doesn't look like she wants to say anything, but instead like she already has and is now awaiting an answer. I am now quite certain that I don't belong in this chair, that she was indeed expecting another—no, not expecting, that another had already been sitting here, invisible, before I came into the kitchen. Am I interrupting? No, I'm not—it's as if Celestina can see the other inside of me, as if the other and I have become one, as if whoever sits in this chair is the other. Celestina continues staring, her eyes neither lifeless nor dead, staring and waiting. Her gaze follows my hand as I finally lift the glass to my lips, take a sip, and savor the first taste of red wine I've had all day—it's as if she's expecting something, some sort of toast, maybe. She's studying me, and her eyes hang on my every move.

I am beginning to grow uneasy. There's a lot to make up for at this point, beginning with my entrance, which placed me on uncertain ground—maybe I shouldn't have gone into the kitchen after all. But now it's done, it's too late: I've landed myself in an unwelcome entanglement, and there's no getting out of it. I pretend to shiver—the opposite, so to speak, of rubbing one's hands together—and say "It's gotten cold."

"Yes," Celestina replies unenthusiastically, nodding her head like an obedient schoolgirl for whom the subject at hand is simply too easy, who was expecting something more challenging, "yes, it has gotten cold." Her articulation is soft and blurred, she is drunker than she appeared at first. "Winter's coming," I say. She says nothing. I try again: "An early winter." "Yes, yes, an early winter," she answers, and then suddenly withdraws into herself as if to assess whether what she just said, and what I just said, is actually true. "An early winter," she repeats; it must have checked out, a permissible statement indeed; I was right, and she nods her head reassuringly, as if I were a child and she my nanny,

and then I start to wonder whether it's really true. Yes, it's
true: even in the kitchen I can feel the early winter spreading through the air. And like every early winter this one is but
another reprise of the first, the original early winter, when there
were still nannies and sleds and muffs and mothballs.

"Yes," says Celestina, and nods once again, bringing the topic
to a close, "but Thy will be done."
    I wait, frozen in place, until a beat has passed and the syl-
lables have died away. Then I look at her, wondering how she
meant it even though I already know—I can feel the realization
rising up from within me, turning to fright, and then to shock,
taking hold of my legs and laming them.
    I reply: "I don't understand what you mean, Celestina," even
though I understand her completely—as they cross my tongue,
the words are clumsy and muddled, ridiculous; I am not even
dressed properly for such statements, in my nightshirt and robe;
I try again: "It is not my will for winter to come earlier this year
than in other years, certainly not!" On the contrary, I think to
myself,

on the contrary, I still wanted to go to Tynset. Tynset—suddenly
it's far away again, unreachable, unapproachable.

What am I getting into here? I lift my glass as if to drink to
Celestina, but even that's not true—what has been said here is
certainly no toast, and what is happening is anything but cele-
bratory. I empty my glass with a single swallow. I must say, this
red wine tastes good—the first glass of the day always tastes the
best, even when one starts drinking as early as I have, in this
kitchen, across from Celestina. I reach for the bottle, which
is standing on the floor under the table—I don't know why
Celestina has put it there. I fill my glass, and then Celestina's.
My hand is trembling, but Celestina doesn't notice; God's hands
never tremble. She lifts the glass to her mouth, drinks, swallows,

sets the glass back down onto the table, and says "Forgive me my sins."

That is outrageous. "With pleasure," I reply in a friendly, but stern tone, indicating my unwillingness to continue playing this game, which is actually anything but a game. "With pleasure, Celestina, but sins are absolutely out of the question, do you hear? Out of the question, really. You have no sins, Celestina, not a single one as far as I know. That said, there is the possibility—I mean, I don't think one can completely rule out the possibility that you drink a little more than you ought, so perhaps you should drink a little less, perhaps—" at which point I realize that I might be lying, maybe she shouldn't drink less—in fact, maybe I should drink more, maybe even as much as Celestina does, but it's too late to say something like that; what's said is said and I can't take it back.

She says "I know you are merciful."

No, we are completely outside of the realm of sanity now: she thinks I'm her god, and that her god is merciful—I wasn't prepared for any of this. I look around. What should I do now? What's my next move?

"Bless me!" she says.

Now, now we've come to this. I have to act, do something. Bless her. How do you bless somebody? True, I did see it once, that time in Rosenheim when the cardinal was there. But I have by no means mastered that sacred gesture, I'm not sure I could even replicate it at all. But even if I could, Celestina is too good to me to warrant such cheap trickery.

"Bless me," says Celestina. Yes, she's drunk, but she is still awake, animated, and completely overcome by the desire to receive my blessing. As I glance around the kitchen my eyes rest for a brief moment on the ticking clock mounted on the wall—it's two in the morning, the chimes have just started ringing. I look at the thermometer on the opposite wall—it displays Reaumur as well as, I believe, Fahrenheit, but I can't see how many degrees. I look at the two copper pots hanging on iron hooks, one of which is very big and the other even bigger—they've always been hanging there. I see a small blue fleck on the wall—that's new, how did that get there?

And now I must return to Celestina, I turn back and face her; her eyes meet mine, but they are agitated now, something is happening inside of her, now she's standing up—no, she's not standing up, but sliding slowly from her chair as if to get down onto her knees. And then, at the last second, she stands after all, staggering and swaying in an inebriated stupor; as she makes her way around the corner of the table, her robe—or whatever it is you call it—catches on the back of the chair, dragging it slowly behind her, scraping against the table until finally it loses its balance and comes crashing down, slamming into the table as it falls to the floor. At this point, Celestina's robe is now stretched across the top of the table, and as she rounds the next corner—how did that blue fleck get there?—it begins clearing the surface of everything in its path; as she lurches forward again, the wine glass topples, those copper pans have hung there for a very long time, it's one minute past two, and a pink pool spills out onto the table, only to be sucked up by her robe, which turns red—it used to be colorless, gray, in Tynset it's gray—wrinkled and wadded like a dish towel drenched in water, it slides across the tabletop—no, only over part of the tabletop; the only part still attached to Celestina are the sleeves, which bunch farther and farther up her arms as she moves; she's now down to her nightgown; the glass rolls across the table, falls, ricochets off of the toppled chair, and shatters into tinkling pieces on the floor; Celestina is now standing in front of me, a heavy mass of drunken flesh in wrinkled white; she falls to her knees—it's now two minutes past two—and begins sliding toward me on the floor; as I watch her doing this, I cannot help but think about her knees, fear for them even; I can feel the pain as the shards of glass cut into her skin—I feel it as if it's my own, despite the fact that the glass fell on the other side of the table; regardless,

I unclench my ankle and make a quick sweeping motion with
my right leg to clear the patch of floor directly in front of me,
where Celestina will shortly be kneeling; she comes closer, slides
closer, how odd this blue fleck is, I wonder how it got there,
there are the pans, still hanging, it's still two minutes after two,
the clock is ticking slower—is it Reaumur or Fahrenheit over
there on the thermometer? I don't want to forget the red wine—
afterwards, later, when this is all over; Celestina sinks down in
front of me, wrapping her arms around my knees; I can feel her
body, heavy and warm and soft, pressed against my shins, the
breasts of a penitent woman, not of a seductress, and at this very
second—it's two and a half minutes past two—the clock stops
ticking, comes to a standstill, causing a stir in the kitchen air; in
the clock's absence the room has become louder, and I can feel
its thickness, drunk with wine and filled with radiating body
heat; I can see the blue fleck on the wall, I can feel Celestina's
hot breath on my knees; as she tilts her head upward I glimpse
moisture in her eyes—they are full of tears—

   —what's happening here? A horrible error, representative of
all other errors I have ever witnessed and not witnessed—

   —I am reminded, for example, of the two men on either side of
Jesus's cross. Who were they anyway? Had they founded their
own religions? They may have been criminals, that's all well and
good—but in whose eyes? How? In the eyes of the same people
who considered Jesus a criminal, or not? Or maybe not? What
kinds of standards are these anyway? Error, caprice, blindness,
from the very beginning,

blindness. Celestina is mumbling—all of a sudden she's gotten
drunker, perhaps she's starting to get delusional as well—mumbling about how I must bless her, bless her now. Now I must
act. Being mistaken for God is not something I can tolerate for
very long—perhaps others can, cardinals, maybe, but I can't. I
won't last much longer.

For the life of me I can't remember how the ritual is per-
formed. How does the movement go again? They all seem to
execute it with such ease, such agility, such economy, but for me
it's gone, forgotten like an old magic trick—hand up, hand here,
hand to the right, to the left, and then in reverse, it's gone—how
do they do it, these holy men, what's the secret to that soft,
supple feat of hand gymnastics that the faithful await with such
longing, that calms them, satisfies them, comforts them, reas-
sures them? How does it go again? I could certainly use it here,
now, on this poor soul; in this hallucinatory trance—you might
even call it ecstasy—she is doubtlessly at her most receptive; and
at this very moment, in this very place, I do believe a deception
of this magnitude would be in order, for it could heal her—

Now—now would be the time to uncover Celestina's secret.
Here she is before me, under me, half naked—there's nothing
she could possibly hide,
    but I will not uncover it, not me; I'm not one to ask ques-
tions, nor am I one to seize the moment. I'm not one of those
Inquisitors who forces his subject to stand naked against the
wall, or in the pillory, and then interrogates him with such
relentless intensity that the questions pierce his skin and stick
from his body like the arrows in St. Sebastian's carcass; nor am
I the father confessor who pinches the tender flesh of young
girls to feel the presence of mortal sin; and I am not a sacred
moralist like that Doctor Liguori, who reaches his hand under
their robes and inserts his fingers between their thighs, probing
their orifices for signs of impurity—no,

she is kneeling before me, kneeling at my feet, and I must look
after her, protect her, make sure that none of these lecherous
men come near her, for she would allow them to do anything
in the hopes that, at last, she might be rid of her sins, the sins
she has not committed.
    Now I realize that I don't even want to know her secret

anymore—it has ceased to interest me. What would I even do with it?

And I will not rob her of her sins either. Then she would be even more naked than she is now, empty, too old to find a replacement for such a great burden. She should stay as she is, a self-proclaimed sinner, a saint.

Away from here!

"Bless me!"

I can no longer remember the correct gesture because I never learned it—I never thought there would come a time when I could use it. I need to find something else to take its place. I bend down toward Celestina and hold her head between my hands; I kiss her moist forehead, stroke her hair, and whisper "I bless you, my child"—or should I have said "my daughter"?

I shouldn't have said anything, at least not that, and I shouldn't have done anything either, at least not what I did. Celestina has figured me out, my voice was not the voice of God, my kiss was not God's kiss, and my words were not the words of the Holy Father—they weren't even the words of a halfway decent priest. All I've succeeded in doing is pushing her further away; now I'm a sinner, or rather, I had been a sinner before and now I am damned—I don't think I was damned before. Celestina looks at me, her eyes are empty, devoid of expression. She stands up. Suddenly she is sober. She runs her hand through her hair and brushes off her knees, looking around the kitchen as if trying to decide where she should begin with her work. She sees my empty wine bottle on the sideboard, opens the cupboard, removes a new bottle, and places it gently—careful not to disturb the sediment—onto the table in front of me.

And with this I know I've been dispatched, I can go; I'm a sinner, maybe even damned, maybe even worse than before, but even the damned have a right to red wine; Celestina doesn't believe it's up to her to administer my punishment—on the Day of Judgment we will appear before the throne hand in hand, at the end of a future that may or may not be very long at all.

And suddenly it's as if I'm not there at all, as if my presence had been nothing more than a momentary draft in the dull kitchen air. Celestina hangs her wet, dripping robe on a wall hook, takes a cloth, moistens it under the faucet, and begins wiping the table clean. After she has finished, she fetches a hand broom and dustpan to clear the shards of broken glass from the floor. She is Celestina at work, sober Celestina, Celestina in the best hours of her day.

I pick up my fresh bottle of wine, stand up, and say "Good night, Celestina," just as I did the night before. And then I leave, shutting the kitchen door behind me—I am no longer God, I am anything but God, I am a nocturnal wanderer in a lonely house.

No sooner have I left the kitchen than my flashlight goes out. I am standing in the cold hallway, on the cold stones in the dark, feeling somewhat stone-like myself. I close my eyes for a moment and then open them again—now it's a little lighter, and I am able to make out a couple of silhouettes here and there, and a couple of surfaces. There is some sort of lightness coming in through the skylight in the loft, which has now made its way to the staircase. It can't be the morning yet—it's 2 a.m. on a November night. Most likely it's the product of the pale harvest moon, of which half, or perhaps a quarter, is currently visible. It's not the summer moon at any rate, not like the one that shines over Bergamo and its white Pierrot, lurching around with his great big sneering mouth, playing his ghastly pranks. No, I am in a dungeon here, in the bowels of the castle in Helsingør, with the king's ghost standing over me. Soon he will be chased off by the crowing of the roosters, or Celestina will mistake him for one of Hell's angels and drive him out.

I feel my way back through the darkness, swaying, toward my bed. It wouldn't make any sense to turn on a light at this point because it would only shine behind me: in each of the rooms I have to pass through to get back to my bedroom there is only one light switch, and as it happens, each of these switches is located on the other side of the room from where I would enter, meaning they are only on the correct side when I'm going in the opposite direction, starting from my bed; for sometimes, not always, when I get up in the night, I want to have light in the house; first, I turn on the lamp on my night table, and then the ceiling light, before opening the door into the empty room directly adjacent; with the brightness from my bedroom lighting my path, I am able to make my way through to the library door, where there is another switch; as I flip it on, the room and its shelves of books spring forth from the darkness, and I proceed into the hall, flipping yet another switch before continuing on my journey, constantly bathed in light; and as I walk from room to room, the trail of luminosity behind me lengthens, my glowing retinue grows brighter, I am detectable, anybody can find me; that is, until I return to my bed, extinguishing the string of lights one by one until the darkness is once again complete and I return to my former state of imperceptibility—

sometimes, however, on nights like tonight, I wish only to illuminate my steps, and to preserve the darkness surrounding the bright circle that hovers a few feet in front of me; I don't want an escort, and I don't want to be recognized so easily by the objects I pass—I would rather surprise them,

but then my flashlight goes out; maybe the objects are revealing their true identities at this very moment, but because I have no light I can't see them; maybe they're laughing at me; I feel my way forward through the crackling dark, taking great care not to be felt myself, for if I were, I would have no way of knowing who or what was feeling me, eventually I'm able to creep back into my bedroom. When I open the door, the lamp on the night table is still burning, illuminating the pad of paper with TYNSET on it. I crawl into bed, pull up the covers, and pick up the pad,

there it stands, TYNSET, threatening to disappear into the thicket of unkempt border decorations. Yes, I wanted to go to Tynset. I would still be interested in going. Interested, yes, but I was much closer to a decision at an earlier point in the night than I am now. After all, we are already quite far into autumn, which means that in Tynset it is likely winter. And not even a particularly early winter for Tynset.

Winter in Tynset? At a way station, in a pension with perhaps twelve or twenty beds made of iron, no running water in the rooms, white shelves with clay jugs full of water that freezes during the nights when the windows are left open. Here it is winter, a cold but clear time under a sparkling sky. On the Day of the Seven Sleepers the potato fields are shrouded in a cloud of icy mist, and on All Souls' Day the town's inhabitants flock to church to repent for the scant sins of summer—not in some ornately decorated sinners' church, but in a surly, puritanical shed, where it reeks of wet fur, wet wood, and wet leather, and where the opening strains of a hymn send a swarm of crows into the air—

Tynset—I would surely go there had experience not taught me that what is closest is never what is best. What's more, it is the unknown Tynset that has taken hold of me so, and who knows whether the real Tynset—what am I even saying, real?—I mean: the material Tynset, built from stone and wood and flesh and blood and thoughts and deeds, whether this Tynset would not evaporate before my eyes or sink into itself like a fata morgana when I approach? And then I would be standing there in utter disappointment—my thoughts would regain a certain freedom, to be sure, but this isn't what they desire anymore;

they've grown unaccustomed to such things. They no longer roam like they used to, but instead have become rooted to the spot, rooted to Tynset.

But I should—I will go, even if it is winter. Tynset, the very name sounds like winter, like the bells of a sleigh coming from somewhere and leaving a trail that I, without feeling bound to any particular direction, decide to follow simply so that I will have a direction, even if it's only to another place where there is nothing to be found and only more to search for; even if it's nothing but a fork or an intersection, setting the stage for a dilemma, a choice between two or possibly many different options. Such a dilemma would be welcome, in fact: I would proceed with deliberate slowness and pedantic care, selecting a path that promises a destination and following it with calm assurance while never losing sight of the possibility that I might, at any time, be led astray; secure in the knowledge that there were other paths I left behind, paths to which I can always return and which will lead me to new forks and new branches, should this particular path ever run out or disappear. All of this, of course, under the condition that I have enough time: a condition I have grown accustomed to incorporating into my plans.

But what's all this talk of plans? I have no plans. The only thing I have is an underdeveloped aim: Tynset. Tynset, the only place for which I would leave my house, and my bed, my winter bed, the white realm—and even then it would be with a heavy heart.

Here I lie, on a cold November night, in the same bed where, on another November night, a murder was committed—

the same bed in which, ten years later, the murderer lay once again, having returned to the scene of the crime, the bed of the crime, without fear of pursuit—his reputation would protect him from that,

the bed in which the murderer, Don Carlo Gesualdo, Prince of
Venosa, spends his final years, agitated, sleepless, detached from
the objects that once populated his life, detached from its passions and from the many varieties of love; he has turned his back
on everything now, even on his sins; reluctantly, discontentedly,
he lifts an eye toward God,

the bed in which the murderer, Don Carlo Gesualdo, spends
his final nights, both eyes now fixed on the heavens, begging
God for forgiveness,

in which the murderer, Don Carlo Gesualdo, spends his final
night, ardently but hopelessly awaiting a word from his creator—

—I'm not trying to say that his creator should have spoken
this word, no, that's not what I'm trying to say at all—

the bed in which the pious Gesualdo spends his final hour,
ethereal, disconnected from the world, from everything, even
from his creator, alone,

spends his final hour, the shifty black eyes in his El Greco
head still glinting as he stares deep into the room, which is not
so much illuminated by torchlight as it is clouded by a silent,
velvety darkness, a heraldic shroud, royal blackness, the likes
of which mere peasants will never know. A coat of arms hangs
over the doorframe, and a halberd is leaning diagonally across
the entrance, placed there by the guard who is sleeping on the
floor directly below,

lying and listening,

and behind him his lute—though it does not rest in the
harmonious, peaceful darkness of a Dutch still life. No, it has
been cast aside in frustration, thrust into its place after a final
cacophonous note, shell facing upward, fingerboard against the
floor, fractious, recalcitrant, a gameboard for his feverish, deadly
fingers, a seismograph of his cruelty, a servant of his capricious
will, his moods,

and in another room, which hasn't been used—or even
entered—for years, lies, with slackened string, the instrument
of his frenzied and erratic hunts: the crossbow,

under the ground near Gesù Nuovo lie his nymphomaniac first wife and her last lover, the Pope's nephew; their desire for one last moment of corporal unity long since frozen in the stillness of death, each skeleton reaches for the other, though it has become difficult to tell now which is which,

and somewhere along his escape route to the east there lies the stiletto, the murder weapon, rusting away

and so, you see, everything is in its place, everything is settled, everything is final,

in the final minutes of his life, he lies in his bed and gazes at the skull under the falling sky—I cannot seem to find the skull; it has disappeared, faded away probably—

he gazes at the skull, and behind the skull there is a light, a deranged flickering which is not actually there because it is inside of him—

as he lies there, he suddenly laughs, and then goes silent again, listening,

but not for his own creation anymore, or his own voices, the soprano, the falsetto, the tenor, and the bass, all of which he used to sing (and not infrequently) because nobody else seemed able to perform at his standards—no, he is no longer listening to himself, the sound of his own voice,

nor is he listening for his dying breath, the whispering, the piercing screams of rapture, the sforzandi, the steep crescendo to paralyzing ecstasy, to the point where beauty is no longer bearable, where death and love coalesce in a singular act of deliverance, where two become one, and where the unexpected becomes unheard of,

nor for the chords, the modulations, harmony and enharmony, the audacious, unabashed, forbidden step from A♭ minor to C major—for he has already taken his last step,

nor does he glide up and down the chromatic scale F, E, E♭, D

o morire—

F, E, D, E, E♭, D, C, B, C
o mori-i-i-re-
—morire, yes, now it is here, but he is not listening for it, not
for death, not for love, not even for God anymore, not for his
crux benedicta, not for these disembodied voices—
     as he lies there in his final moments, he is listening for some-
thing else, something unexpected, but he doesn't hear it, he
doesn't hear anything; he lies with his head here, exactly where
mine is now, and listens into the emptiness, stares into it, and
then dies, the immortal, the incomprehensible, the great one, the
mystery, the miracle, the murderer, *inter mortuos liber*, here, in
this very bed, the winter bed, where I am lying at this moment
on a cold November night.

I hear steps in the house.
     They belong to Celestina. She has just finished cleaning the
kitchen, and now she is heading up to her bedroom, a candle in
one hand, a bottle of wine in the other, mounting each step in
silent agitation, ensnarled in her sins; and as she continues on
her way, through the cold darkness of the early morning, her
hopes of redemption vanish like fog lifting from the path of a
solitary wanderer.

Celestina: the greatest trial in our relationship had been early
on, shortly after I had taken over direction of the house, and
consequently, of her. There used to be an apple tree nearby,
which nobody had bothered to fell despite the fact that it had
not borne fruit—or even green leaves—for some years. But one
day the leaves returned, followed shortly by luscious blossoms
promising a bountiful crop. During the weeks over which this
reawakening took place, Celestina did not utter a single word
to me, and took my directions with a stony countenance and
averted eyes. One time, after I had finished speaking to her, I
happened to turn back around, only to find her crossing herself.

Naturally, suspicions of witchcraft would have served as a perfect opportunity to seek the guidance of a priest, to open the church doors again—even if just a crack—and reenter the community to which she so desperately yearned to belong, but Celestina did not take it. At some point she must either have forgiven me of forgotten the incident entirely,

and even though the late summer's crop was magnificent, each bite a bacchanalian feast, crisp and succulent like the apples from the Tree of Knowledge, Celestina did not eat a single one.

That was ten or eleven years ago, and after that one summer the tree never produced again. Eventually it died off, and I had it cut down—who knows, perhaps it would have come back to life if I had let it stay, but for Celestina's sake I didn't want it to.

A mystery. Or at least: part of the great mystery— —

—now I am growing tired—

part of the great mystery called Tynset. Now I am very tired. Yes, Tynset is a good name for the mystery. By giving the unknown a name, it automatically becomes more familiar—the answer is not revealed through naming, but at least you can call it something, at least it has a label, something with which to summarize and encipher the mysterious element; and TYNSET is the sum of them all, as well as their root. It's a good name, I think, fitting, or at least the best I was able to come up with.

But what do I even think Tynset is? What? —Nothing, be quiet, nothing. A secret is hiding back there. Perhaps a journey wouldn't even be the best way to find it. At least not right now. Later, yes, later, if everything else fails, perhaps later, when my fingers grow cold and stiff, when I grow tired and the light shining on my train of thought goes dark, later, when the words trickle away, when I can no longer find the pearls in the books, or the nothingness behind the Milky Way, when I can no longer feel the cold wind, when there is no more air; only then would there be nothing left, and perhaps then I would summon the last of my strength and strike out. But until then I must keep that point inside, reserving it for the right moment. I must also never lose sight of it. I should be happy that I found this name without ever having searched for the place or the thing that bears it. Some names are so beautiful that attempting to decipher their meaning invariably leads to a false paradise, a forest of foolish indulgence with a mossy floor of sweet dreams on which unicorns lightly prance, while others are so laden down with memories that it's impossible to banish the original owners from my mind, to free myself from their merciless presence. To find a name that is neither of these things is rare. With Tynset, though—and this is becoming clearer and clearer to me—I think of nothing, nothing and nobody, except for Hamlet, but I think about him a lot; I was thinking about him even before I found Tynset, and it is possible that without him, Tynset would not have stayed with me as it has. True, I often digress, but that does not mean I have let go. There are times when Tynset escapes me, but it always comes back, and above all, it keeps growing, constantly expanding onto the white of my notepad,

standing there, alone, Tynset stands alone, and there is nothing more to come, no explanation, no commentary—I will even free it from the decorations I have added to its border, for they are threatening to overtake it. Doing so will also serve to restore its pathos, but then again, I don't think it ever really lost it, Tynset.

I write it out again; there it is, now it is, like so much else, a large heading with nothing below, nothing but white paper. Maybe it should be like that? I'll wait and see—I'm tired—I lay the notebook back down—what was I thinking of before? What was it? Tynset—nothing—be quiet, nothing—I will sleep now— — —

Fortnum & Mason, 111–119 Piccadilly, London, W1, blends one, two, and three—

van der Veersschoutte & Klijnstra, 113 Prinsengracht, Amsterdam, blends one and three—

Alberto Sackpfühde Jr., Hamburg 2, 24 Alter Wall, blends two and three—

—blend one, no deliveries within Germany, yes, "deliveries" is the word. Rosemary doesn't seem to carry much appeal for the Germans, neither does garlic,

German eaters place a great deal of importance on the purity of breath. Who was it who said that to me? A man with a thick, sturdy neck, whom I found myself sitting across from in the dining car. Later, I saw his picture in the newspaper, his name was Jerka, or Jörka—if I remember correctly, he had removed the hip bones from a couple of Danish men during the war and transplanted them into Germans, quite an accomplishment in his field—

but away from this field now; I wanted to sleep, and I was close to doing so: Traitteur Schwendimann, Zürich, 7 Seilergraben, blends one, two, and three—

Ditta Luigi Rigamonti, 88 via Rossini, Milano, blends one, two, and three—

yes, all unknown, all present—no danger of forgetting here—

Giuliano Rho S., c/o, 14 via Archimede, Milano, blends one, two, and three—

Gianfrancesco Ravagnan, Zattere 1044 — — — —

—I awake once again, washed up onto the threshold of the night, the place where the web of darkness thins and light begins to sprinkle through the gaps and crevices, where it is not yet clear which of the two adversaries will step aside, who will relinquish the great battlefield. I look at the clock. It is twenty minutes before four. I will simply pass the time until daylight,

but I have not yet let go of the night; I am holding her, and now that I have her, my grip tightens, my eyes stay shut; clinging to the first small shred I can reach, I pull myself hopelessly along behind her, grunting with exertion as my feet drag along the earth behind me.

I can't have slept very long; it has perhaps been a half hour

since I was last awake, or even less than that—the tranquility
of slumber had not yet enveloped my body, and the waves have
not stopped crashing; I can still feel the receding day in my
fingertips, despite the fact that it is long since passed and has
left no traces; I can feel it in my toes as well—in the moment
of my waking I can feel it tingling in the tips of my outermost
extremities and stirring in the deepest depths, and now that I
am awake, it stirs anew, making its way toward the middle like
ripples in reverse, shooting back to the epicenter, where the stone
first plunged through the surface, and within seconds I am a
quaking island in an ocean of stillness. And so I lie there in the
darkness, the commotion building and building inside me, I lie
there and listen. But to what? To the oscillations of what may
have awakened me. From the silence there arises a pulsating
hum, and my heart begins to throb as if it wants nothing more
than to burst through the walls of my body, to get out, just
out—but other than this I hear nothing, not even the roosters,
for they have gone quiet. So I know it was not a noise that
roused me but a sudden shift, one that took place somewhere
at this exact moment, perhaps here in my room—no, not here,
nothing ever stirs here; perhaps out there, on the other side
of the window, perhaps there is a man with a long shadow, a
murderer even, crouching on the ground and preparing to jump
up to my window ledge, or perhaps at the streetlight on the
corner, standing and waiting for another who will never arrive,
or maybe even farther away, maybe in Tynset or some other
removed corner of the earth, or even farther, in space perhaps.
At this very moment, something is being born, emerging; it
may be something terrifying, but it just as easily may not be;
perhaps it is something that will become terrifying, something
that, over a long period of time—so long, even, that I may not
live to see its end—will grow to be deadly, just as we carry our
causes for death deep within us, like a swallowed piece of bait, a
hook from which nothing can free us but another cause, another
lure, or, in some cases, an external force. Perhaps, in some hole

or crevice in the rocks, in the atmosphere or somewhere among the planets, a silent shift is taking place, a seemingly harmless shift, whose presence will be sensed by a person born this very hour, but whose horrific effects will not become apparent until much later in life. Perhaps it is a system of high pressure from the Atlantic, or low pressure from the Mediterranean—I've forgotten which comes from where—the weather's changing of the guard, or perhaps an earthquake in Lisbon or Sicily, like the one Goethe felt in the seismographic bones under the mass of his Olympian flesh—no, not that, not Sicily, not Lisbon, from my current vantage point, looking into the night, these places don't even exist. I am in another dimension entirely.

Whatever it is, though, it's inalterable, and I'm no match for it—there is certainly no way I can face it wearing just this nightshirt. I am completely at its mercy, as I am at the mercy of everything. I lie motionless on my back, in this bed, my winter bed, looking up with blind eyes and seeing nothing, relinquishing myself to horror, ready for anything; and then I am loose again, my limbs relax, my tendons slacken, and I feel my body sink back down into the mattress—the bolster—I allow myself to be drawn toward the center of the earth, testing the force of its pull, savoring it as I sink deeper and deeper, enveloped by the burning desire to be swallowed whole, to be a part of the earth, flush with its surface, so that everything, bodies, wind, and time, would simply pass me by. The pulsing in my blood begins to fade and my heart brings its wings to rest, folding them loosely together like a wild pheasant readying itself for the cold of night. There remains a faint humming in my blood, but the tone has ceased to oscillate, and the waves are growing weaker, flatter, smoother, and

in the distance a cloud is gathering, and dark shapes assemble into hordes of cursed thoughts, forming a dream that slowly begins its advance, picking up speed as it goes, its banners whipping in the wind, ready to besiege my mind and vivify my sleep, its horrors shielding me from the horrors of the outside, before passing over me as I lie deep in my grave, asleep once again, beneath it all

and awake in a fit of laughter, or rather the memory of laughter. We laughed a lot back then, she and I. We were sitting in some dive—I can't remember if it was in the north or the south—and in came an athlete with immense arms and bracelets to boot. He specialized in ripping telephone books. And rip them he did, one after the other, right before our eyes—and not lengthwise but straight across. After a while, he was standing up to his knees in shredded telephone books, and we had to laugh.

Who was the person with whom I spent two or three summers in Somerset, among rolling hills covered with pristine meadows and hemmed by tranquil pastures, a straight-lined, thoroughly planned, perfectly ordered landscape—as far as the eye could see, every inch of it had been meticulously sketched out and decorated by architects of the Baroque, who left nothing to chance, not even the stormy clouds rolling through the sky. To them, the land was a stage, and this the performance of a lifetime, an apotheosis. And then the storm arrived, and stayed with us until evening. By nightfall it had passed, swept away by a gust of wind, and suddenly all of the curtains started billowing inward—a catharsis, the stale air of an entire life washed away in an instant. The next morning nothing was the same. We walked through the park, talking about something I no longer remember. The park was clear, damp, and cool, its lines sharper, as if pressing for a decision.

—or that time in the labyrinth, the calls, the echoes in the gardens; we were young then, back there in the labyrinth, and we chased each other about in the fading light. And then the watchman stepped out onto the balcony with his dog, a frighteningly repulsive animal, like the dog in the frescos in the Camera degli Sposi—were dogs really that ugly during the Renaissance, or was it simply that Renaissance artists couldn't paint them?

—or the passages in October or November, many years ago, the guttural screams of the gulls circling the mast as it rocked back and forth in the wind like a giant metronome keeping the tempo of the waves—

we were drawing nearer—we are drawing nearer to the white chalk cliffs of Dover, or we are drifting away, Kronborg Castle emerges on the shores of Helsingør, or it disappears, swept away like a ghost in the wind as Hamlet's father rides by on a broomstick—there was also a green coast, that was Cornwall, and above us a flag was flapping in the wind, and her hair was blowing. She was wrapped in a long, woolen shawl—but whose shawl was it, and whose hair? Whose eyes? She was wearing sunglasses, but not because it was sunny, for it was not sunny, the sky was—

yes, the sky was gray, dark gray, like the color of tin. It was a sky that, for fear of limiting its possibilities, would not decide, while its capricious impulses floated by overhead in dark wisps, blue gaps, and pale mist. Yes, she was wearing sunglasses because the water was splashing and spraying against the hull, leaving a salty crust on the lenses. At some point she turned to me and shouted something over the wind—

—at some point, as we sat on the bench in the park, she turned to me and asked me a question. I don't remember anymore what she asked or how I answered—

—at some point we suddenly ran into each other in the labyrinth at the Villa Barbarigo. I remember it was as if we had just seen each other for the first time face to face—

yes, of course, it was the same person each time. But who was it? What was her name?

"Damn braces: bless relaxes"—who said that again? I believe it was Blake. Yes, it was Blake—he knew it, but I knew it better. I will never master the craft. I have looked into their studios—I understand the temperament of the masters. What evades me is a foothold: before my very eyes I watch as meaning turns to vapor, revealing the meaninglessness behind it. These are simply not things that I can grasp, hold on to—and he who falls where others climb should not pull the others down with him.

I wanted to sleep. No, I wanted to go to Tynset, but not by train. By car instead. I should listen to the road conditions report—is that what it's called? Yes, the road conditions report, that's it. I should look up the number first, in the telephone book, otherwise it will just be those women again with their roux and their heaps of flour—

the park in the storm, the calls and the echoes in the labyrinthine gardens—
     one—
the Gonzagas' dog, and the wild screeching of the gulls,
     six—
the road is leading upward, swinging from curve to curve like a pendulum, before the snowdrifts, through clouds of fog and patches of wind—
     nine—
the fog lights flow out over the snow, yellow, scanning the frozen white walls alongside the road, the tire chains fling barely frozen slush from the road, still not there, not yet—

the following passes have been closed until further notice—closed, you say. So there we have it, the early winter, it's coming, and soon it will be here—*Juchten, Pelagonier, Septimer, Julier, Pelegrin*—I would like to drive over all of these, ever upward, deeper into the snow, farther and farther—*Pordoi-Joch iced over, Persenner Steige iced over, Lukmanier iced over*—iced over or not, I can drive over ice, and I will travel every road, ever upward—*hard snow up to two thousand meters, then becoming powdery. The following passes have been cleared: Fuorn Sugana Tellina*—I will cross the threshold from hard snow to powder, ever upward, pushing off, gliding—*passes that have been cleared are only drivable with snow chains. Caution: only one lane is clear at this time*—one lane or two, it doesn't matter; I will lift off from the road and fly—*heavy fog above fifteen hundred meters*—I will cut through the fog—*especially at night*—I will cut through the night, floating, flying, upward, ever upward, heading once again for the stars, again and again, to the hole in the Milky Way, driving and driving, through the hole again, to the place where there is nothing more—driving into nothing—nothing

—yes, I have just managed to glimpse the tail of the fading night. It seems that way, at least. I was sleeping. Now the night is over, although I did manage to hold on to a small sliver of it before it vanished completely. Be that as it may, I am now awake, not wide awake, but awake, awake enough that I'm no longer thinking about sleep. It is light.

Something has happened. This is not the light of a conventional day, but the light of an unconventional one, a sickly white light, pale, yet blinding, a daytime specter floating through my room and reflecting in my windows, making the walls flicker. The windows are vertical rectangles with bars like fish bones, a skeleton of muted, dark white that splits the brightness streaming through the panes into eight dislocated squares. And everything's quiet, quieter than when I normally awake, as if all the sounds have been choked. What was it that woke me up? I listen inside and then out, but I hear nothing, the neighbor's rooster has long since stopped crowing, and I haven't heard the second rooster for days now. It's light, and they are tending to their hens, like all the roosters in all the countries where it is light.

Nothing awakened me save for the end of the night and the exceptional, excruciating light of this unconventional day. And now, all of a sudden, I know. I can feel it in my limbs, I know what woke me earlier and what has awoken me now, what frightened me during my wakeful hours at night, and why it's now so incredibly bright in my bedroom. It's snowing, and there's already snow on the ground. That's it, that's more than enough to do it. It has unexpectedly turned to winter. Unexpectedly? No, I was ready for the early winter, I even told Celestina about it, before I—before I gave her my blessing, or rather, before I tried to.

And Tynset? What about Tynset?

Gone, finished. It's too late. No more about that. In snow like this I never would have gotten to Tynset, never. In any case, I very likely promised myself too much, although I cannot seem to remember what it was that I promised. It had to have been something. For whatever it actually is, though, there are many things it cannot be, for there have been many times when I've allowed myself to indulge in illusions and false hopes. It will not be with a sense of fulfillment that I reach this place, but nor will it be with a sense of dismay. Dismay is not tied to any one place, it knows no location—instead, it spreads through time and is everywhere at once. In some places it is invisible, but it is still there, still everywhere—and though it hides, it also grows, flourishes, blooms, and bears fruit.

A long time ago I saw a mother and her child walking down the street. All of a sudden the child stumbled and fell to the ground. It was not injured, it did not scream, it didn't even cry—in fact, it didn't make any sound whatsoever; there wasn't even a trace of fright in its face, no pain, no fear; its eyes remained open but were expressionless, a book without words; its mouth was closed and unmoving. But it did not get up. The child's mother tried to lift it from the ground, but her efforts were countered with the full force of youthful strength as the child resisted being moved from its spot, lying there in the street, in the dirt, uninjured, silent, and wide-eyed. Finally, with one last labored heave, the mother succeeded in lifting the child back onto its feet and brushing the grime from its clothes. Now that it was standing again, the child did not resist, and allowed its mother

to lead the way, following silently and blankly as she continued down the street. I watched the child as they passed me by,
and the child met my gaze—and for a brief moment our lives
were traveling side by side. After the child passed where I was
standing, it turned and looked at me, its gaze locking with mine
once again. And then it was over. The child turned its back and
I turned mine, both of us going our separate ways. As I walked
away, I turned around one last time to look, and at the very same
moment I saw the child do the same. After that, I never saw it
again. I don't even remember if it was a girl or a boy—probably
a boy, but no matter what it was, I love this child.

I lift the covers from my body, surrendering the warmth of my
short sleep. As I sit up and slide over to the edge of the bed,
slipping blindly into my slippers, I feel a new kind of cold, much
different than the one I experienced during the night when I
thought it was autumn. The winter spreads out over the floor,
engulfing my feet in an icy mist and billowing over the thresh-
olds as it creeps from room to room, swallowing my possessions
one by one.

I go to the window and peer out into the night. The sky is
not clear, but is shrouded in dark gray, like a giant sieve sprin-
kling white flakes that spiral and wave about as they fall toward
the earth, like feathers from the mattress of Mother Hulda, the
most frightful of all childhood deities. It is an occurrence that
always surprises me. How often will it continue to surprise me?
It always makes me think of that Venezuelan mestiza who died
upon seeing snow for the first time—whereupon the rest of her
clan, gripped by equal measures of terror and humility, knelt to
the ground and prayed to their god, fully expecting to be dealt
the same fateful blow.

The church bells sound nine—even they have been dampened by the snow. The tones have a muffled, wooly quality upon
reaching my ears, and it is almost impossible to hear the initial strike. All that remains is a horrible vibration that glides

through the air, radiating in waves from its source. There are no reverberations, just a trembling diminuendo at the edge of the mountains, where sound and echo are forced together, colliding and jostling with one another until they finally die away, such dreadful music.

I go back to the bed, slip my slippers off, lie down, and pull the covers back up to my chin—and with that the prelude to my day has come to an end, or perhaps even the main theme; now I must await the variations, and maybe at the end there will be a fugue. Tynset? No, not that, not a fugue.

At this point one of the church bells begins tolling again, but it is a different bell from before. There is at least one ringing at most times during the day—only rarely does the bell tower go completely silent. There are a total of five bells, I think to myself, or maybe six, and at least one of them is always on duty. Is today a holiday? Perhaps it is a commemoration of the Temptation of St. Anthony, but as far as I know, that isn't until December 2, and we haven't come that far yet. Besides, a celebration of that magnitude would certainly warrant a larger bell. The one I hear at the moment is small, perhaps even the smallest of the lot, its tone is bright, metallic, and mournful. They call this bell "Stella Mariä." I don't know why they call it that. Once every year—in May, I believe—it is christened by a group of young girls who have not yet taken their first Communion. Beforehand they must bathe and go to confession. Dressed in immaculate white, with collars of lace and metal necklaces with bone crucifixes hung around their necks, strings of flowers running through their hair, they sing dismal tunes about the insignificance of all earthly things in the face of eternal salvation, which they—according to the songs, at least—await with fervor and joyful self-abnegation. Stella Mariä does not chime hours, but seconds, falling into complete silence between each strike like a metronome set at Grave—no, more like a very slow heartbeat. It sounds something like this: Bim—sound fades into a second of silence—Bim—second—Bim—second—and so on.

But this is a death. A child has died. For adults there is a different set of bells, a pair, in fact: one for women and one for men. And the more important the deceased's role in society, the longer the tolling will last. Recently I was walking on the Piazza when the bells began sounding for a man. And the entire crowd stood still—no, it was more that they came slowly to a halt, as if the clockwork driving their legs had gradually worn itself out; as they stood there, they listened, their necks arched backward and their eyes fixed on the top of the tower, anxious to find out if the duration of the tolling would confirm their suspicion that it was the mayor this time, whose broken heart had left him in a vulnerable state of health. Depending on the views and social position of the onlooker, his death would either be a cause for worry or for hope. But the tolling did not last—it turned out to be just a farmer. And as the last note died away and the certainty of no further tolling began to spread across the square, certainty that the mayor had evaded his fate once again, the clockwork slowly set itself back into motion; the people continued on their way and went about their business, exchanging one final glance as they passed each other, a lifeless glance, but one that was drawn taut with meaning, that said: not this time, but next time for sure, soon it will be his turn, and maybe even yours.

But this time it is just a child. The bells have already stopped tolling, which means it wasn't even an important child, probably belonged to a farmer, and a poor one at that—

Celestina—what will she do when she sees me tomorrow? And what will I do?

I'll ask Celestina, she knows these things, and never needs to ask for herself. She knows who will die early, and who will die late, who doesn't have much time left, who can't keep on living, who won't get far, who will grow old, who will be taken into the arms of God, and who will be scorned. She knows a great deal, Celestina.

At any rate, the funeral is scheduled for eleven o'clock. Funerals are always scheduled for eleven so that the reception afterward will begin around noon. The path to the cemetery is a good fifteen minutes of gentle but steady uphill walking, and the path back another fifteen, going downhill—in other words, burials make you hungry, set the stomach a-rattling. Finally seated at the table, the mourners unfold their napkins and rub their hands hungrily together. The atmosphere is fraternal, grave, muted, proper, and each of them feels humbled by the immense power of destiny: while one of them lies beneath the ground, the others have been granted a delicious meal, although it very well may be their last.

I will go to the funeral at eleven and accompany the child, whose name I do not know, to its final resting place. I am certain there will not be very many people in attendance—after all, it was only a farmer's child—especially in weather like this, snow, which is forming drifts now, and frigid cold. It will be a pitifully small procession, a densely packed mass trudging through the snow in black and gray; only the little girls, the child's schoolmates, will be dressed in white, snow-white in the snow, distinguishable from the background only by the red of their cheeks and the black of their hymnals. They will likely have been told that their friend is now celebrating his union with the baby Jesus, with the Christ child, an angel that will continue to watch over all of them and keep record of their good deeds. They will run in front of the priest, who, surrounded by pubescent choirboys with cracking voices, will swing the basin of holy water slowly from side to side, the pointed sleeves of his robe following slightly behind, in the rhythm of his measured footsteps, to the right, to the left, to the right, to the left, like a heavy bell, with the small band of attendants huddled closely behind him like a pack of house pets following a dish piled high with pungent food. Each member of the procession will be carrying an umbrella, doing his or her part to reconcile the sacredness of the act with the dreariness of reality. And they are right to do so—for of all of reality's dreary facets, death is by far the dreariest, the ambassador of dreariness. One should treat death as one treats a state official, an officer of the law, or a tax collector: as a bothersome and entirely unnecessary evil, not even deserving of a conversation, neither glamorous nor majestic; merely a tool in the hand of another; not the helmsman, but the craft itself—I shall drain the wind from its sails. I will go to the funeral, I will perhaps go to the funeral—not on account of death, however, but on account of the dead, even if it is just a child, to strengthen its following by one more attendant, one who has thought the matter through and who knows what it is about, which, by the way, is nothing, absolutely nothing. I will accompany them with my head bowed, I will join the troupe of poverty-stricken mourners—when I think about Mozart's death—

There was not a single attendee at Mozart's burial, not even Constanze, who was bed-ridden with a cold. In fact, the coffin didn't even make it to the grave that day, for no grave had been dug. It didn't make it to the cemetery either, for the cemetery was closed: since there appeared to be nobody on the schedule the gravediggers had gone out drinking and such. And so Mozart was hastily buried by the side of the road—he had always been a man of small stature, and his corpse was even smaller, shriveled from a violent heat rash—stuffed in some tiny hole with the aid of a sturdy boot sole, and covered by the falling snow. This is how it happened. Did they have umbrellas back then?

When was the umbrella invented? I should jot this question down, perhaps, for it is truly a question to which there is an answer—to which there should be an answer— —

Umbrellas: when I was in London, I once saw a performance of *Hamlet* with modern costuming, as they call it, and at Ophelia's funeral everybody, King Claudius, Queen Gertrude, and the

whole band of villains, was carrying an umbrella. For me, this
heightened sense of realism, which even went so far as to take the
weather into account, was very effective. At some point during
the performance, Hamlet had to sneeze, and as he did so, a wave
of speculation swept through the audience: was it the actor who
had caught a cold, or was it Hamlet himself? Was this just an
unfortunate fluke, or had it been the intention of the director all
along? But when Hamlet sneezed once again, and immediately
thereafter began awkwardly fishing around in his pocket for a
handkerchief, in which he loudly and resolutely blew his nose,
we knew immediately: this had been a creative decision on the
part of the director, an attempt to bring us closer to Hamlet's
humanity, his physical vulnerability, to show us that even he,
the sufferer, the chosen one, is a slave to his mortal features.
There followed an immediate round of applause, which came
as somewhat of a shock to the actor, who was now uncertain
whether or not he should sneeze a third time; his execution had
been spot on—not only had he presented us with a perfect imi-
tation of an acute head cold, but the interjection of the sneeze
had acted as an enticing caesura in the escalation of Hamlet's
deadly dilemma. In the end he decided not to repeat it, which
was probably the correct decision: in the blink of an eye this
small, well-placed gesture, this subtle nod to the connoisseurs
had been wiped away, allowing the action to proceed. He was
a very good Hamlet indeed, or at least: as good as an actor can
possibly be when trying to portray Hamlet.

Now I remember: her name was Vanessa. Vanessa, a good name.
And I must have loved her. I remember—
     I remember how sometimes, in the dark night, I would lean
closely over her sleeping figure—nearly paralyzed by fear for her
life—so I could listen for the sound of her breath.
     Is she still breathing?

Tynset. In weather like this, in a snowstorm like this, which grows worse and worse as one travels northward, intensifying, falling thicker, gusting more violently, straightening walls, I would have been stopped in my tracks, probably before I had even reached the pass, before I had turned onto the larger road, or maybe even at the last pass, or at the next one, or the one after that, or even in the flatlands. No, the snow is already too high to drive. Tynset is moot. Now I will never be able to get there, and never again will I even try. I will never even leave this house again—and why should I anyhow?—I also won't be going to the funeral, for even if I did I would not be paying the child any respect, not anymore—it wouldn't even know I was there. But death, death would take note, the scoundrel. He would think I had come to pay *him* my respects, which would certainly not have been the case—no, most certainly not.

I will let Tynset go, forget it, repress it, yes, I will abandon the game and the riddle and treat it like pure chance, like everything is in perfect order. And to do so, I don't even need to stand up—I can remain right where I am, lying in my winter bed,

in the bed of age-old passions and infidelities, of double murder and lonely death, where secrets and horrors have left depressions in the mattress, where a mysterious, inimitable murderer once lay,

a murderer, but not a defender of the Order or a spreader of reddish yellow hands, no skinner, no retiree from Schleswig-Holstein, and no bone-breaking patriarch from Vienna, no hangman, no shooter,

in this bed of winter nights, of moonlit nights, of dark nights, the bed in which I am lying yet again, deep under the covers despite the light of day, the bed in which I will lie forever and from which I will let Tynset disappear—I can see it fading into the distance, it is already far away, and now it is gone, the name forgotten, swept up by the wind, like an echo, like smoke, like a final breath—

WOLFGANG HILDESHEIMER (December 9, 1916–August 21, 1991) was a German writer, dramatist, and painter known for his contributions to the so-called Theater of the Absurd as well as his inventive treatments of the biographical genre. He was born in Hamburg but studied and worked in England and Palestine before returning to Germany to serve as an interpreter in the Nuremberg Trials. He later became associated with the acclaimed *Gruppe 47* and in 1957 settled in Poschiavo, Switzerland, where he spent the remaining years of his life.

JEFFREY CASTLE is a literary translator and PhD candidate at the University of Illinois at Urbana-Champaign.